PARK FOREST PUBLIC LIBRARY
3 1139 00557 3471

P9-BYN-796

WITHDRAWN

A Lowcountry Christmas

Also by Mary Alice Monroe and available from Center Point Large Print:

A Lowcountry Wedding
The Summer's End

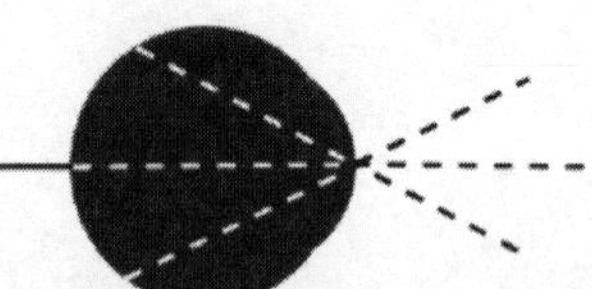

This Large Print Book carries the Seal of Approval of N.A.V.H.

A Lowcountry Christmas

WITHDRAWN

Mary Alice Monroe

CENTER POINT LARGE PRINT
THORNDIKE, MAINE
PARK FOREST PUBLIC LIBRARY 60466

This Center Point Large Print edition is published
in the year 2017 by arrangement with Gallery Books,
a division of Simon & Schuster, Inc.

Copyright © 2016 by Mary Alice Monroe, Ltd.

All rights reserved.

This book is a work of fiction. Any references to historical events, real people, or real places are used fictitiously. Other names, characters, places, and events are products of the author's imagination, and any resemblance to actual events or places or persons, living or dead, is entirely coincidental.

The text of this Large Print edition is unabridged.
In other aspects, this book may vary
from the original edition.
Printed in the United States of America
on permanent paper.
Set in 16-point Times New Roman type.

ISBN: 978-1-68324-226-0

Library of Congress Cataloging-in-Publication Data

Names: Monroe, Mary Alice, author.
Title: A lowcountry Christmas / Mary Alice Monroe.
Description: Center Point Large Print edition. | Waterville, Maine : Center Point Large Print, 2017.
Identifiers: LCCN 2016043657 | ISBN 9781683242260 (hardcover : alk. paper)
Subjects: LCSH: Large type books. | Christmas stories.
Classification: LCC PS3563.O529 L685 2017 | DDC 813/.54—dc23
LC record available at https://lccn.loc.gov/2016043657

This book is for *my* Marine—my son
Zachary Oscar Werner Kruesi.
You inspire me and make us proud.

JAN 1 1 2017
DIRECT

Acknowledgments

Thank you first to my readers. You have been so gracious and kind to me over the years, I want to express how much I appreciate your letters, comments, gifts, your word-of-mouth, and for coming to meet me when I'm on book tour. I read every letter and they encourage me while writing. I hope you will enjoy this gift of a book, written with much love for you for the holidays.

Much love and gratitude to all the booksellers who invite me to their wonderful stores and introduce or recommend my books to new readers.

I am always grateful for the brilliant insights and encouragement offered by my editor and friend, Lauren McKenna—but for this book especially we both worked so hard and so close because we loved this story so much. Also many thanks (and congrats!) to Elana Cohen, to Marla Daniels, and Steve Boldt for all your careful edits and the quick turnaround. And to my glorious publishers, Louise Burke, Jennifer Bergstrom, and Jennifer Long, for your continued gracious and wholehearted support. I have the best team at Gallery and I appreciate all the magic you do every day. Thank you Liz Psaltis, Kristin Dwyer, Jean Anne Rose, Diana Velasquez, and Mackenzie Hickey. Love to Gallery Books!

At Trident Media Group I'm sending heartfelt thanks and praise to my agents, Kimberly Whalen and Robert Gottlieb. Thank you for all you've done these past years. And special thanks to Phoebe Cramer.

Heartfelt gratitude, love, and holiday best wishes to my stellar home team, who work with such enthusiasm and love—my treasured assistant, Angela May; the dynamic duo at Magic Time Literary Group, Kathie Bennett and Susan Zurenda; Meghan Walker at Tandem Literary Group; and Steve Bennett and the team at Authorbytes. Thank you for all you do.

To my L.F. copyeditors, Leah Greenberg and Judy Boehm—we'll always have Maine!

As always, I couldn't write my books without the invaluable help from experts in the fields I am researching. First, continued thanks to the fabulous team at the Dolphin Research Center, Florida. Working with the DRC's Project Odyssey for Wounded Warriors (which I wrote about in *The Summer Wind*), I became acquainted with servicemen and their service dogs. Since then I've talked to many organizations across the United States that provide trained service dogs to returning veterans suffering from PTSD and/or traumatic brain injury. I am in awe of the life-changing work they do. I was particularly intrigued by the groups that rescued dogs from shelters to train, thus demonstrating the great dogs that await adoption. This win-win scenario deserves our continued gratitude and support. I was especially inspired by Clarissa Black and the amazing group she founded, Pets for Vets, a national organization. With her permission, I used her name as a character. All mistakes are my own! Heartfelt thanks to Debra Manos, whose vast experience training dogs helped me appreciate the incredible bond of trust between dog and human.

Thanks to Luis Carlos Montalván, author of *Until Tuesday* and the children's books *Tuesday Takes Me There* and *Tuesday Tucks Me In*. His insights into the struggles of PTSD and his connection with his service dog—and deep, abiding love—were brilliant and inspired me throughout the writing of my novel. To Luis, my son Zachary Kruesi, and to all the men and women who served and currently serve our country, a humble thank-you for your service.

A special nod to Stuart McDaniel, who supported the Center for Birds of Prey in Awendaw, South Carolina (the site of my novel *Skyward*) with his bid for me to create a character named after his grandson Miller McDaniel. The character of the young boy came to life in my mind with great affection and I hope the real Miller likes his namesake!

I have friends who are always a text, phone call, or hug away. You know who you are. I can't say thank you enough or tell you too often how much

I appreciate your constant support while I'm under deadline. I love you all!

As with all my books, I end by expressing my deepest love, appreciation, and thanks to my family, who are my rock during my long hours of writing. First and foremost to my husband, Markus Kruesi, who pulled extra duty this year with driving me on book tour and for preparing endless meals, guarding my privacy as I wrote, and reminding me that I'm loved. To Gretta Kruesi and Jordan Konow, who covered animal duty without complaint whenever I had to leave town; to Zack Kruesi for answering all my questions concerning the Marine Corps; and to Caitlin and Wesley Kruesi for your constant love. To Jack Dwyer for advising me on dialogue and all things pertaining to my young boy character, and to Claire, John, Teddy, and Delancey Dwyer for your ever-present support, love, and encouragement. You are "home" to me. I am the luckiest wife and mother in the world.

Peace and love to all!

Author's Note

The character Taylor McClellan is familiar to those who read the Lowcountry Summer Trilogy and *A Lowcountry Wedding*. Taylor was a Wounded Warrior in the novels. His character is inspired by a serviceman I met while working with the Wounded Warrior Project Odyssey at the Dolphin Research Center. He took the time to share with me why his service dog meant so much to him and stayed by his side. As he spoke, his hand was on his dog's head and neck, stroking and petting as a touchstone. I could readily see the strong connection between them and was inspired.

Post-traumatic stress disorder (PTSD), sometimes known as shell shock or combat stress, occurs after the experience of severe trauma or a life-threatening event. It's normal for the mind and body to be in shock after such an event, but this normal response becomes PTSD when the nervous system gets "stuck."

Veteran suicide rates have reached twenty-two per day according to the Department of Veterans Affairs. Fifty percent of those with PTSD do not seek treatment.

Scientific research is just beginning on whether service dogs actually help treat PTSD and its symptoms. Anecdotal reports, however, are clear.

Veterans vividly describe how service dogs have helped them recover from PTSD when they could not find relief from other interventions. Service dogs provide support and increased means of coping with such symptoms as hypervigilance, fear, nightmares, the fight-or-flight response, and impaired memory.

A common link in my novels is the connection we share with animals. Witnessing the connection between service dogs and their masters is extraordinarily powerful. I've wanted to write about this unique bond for years. At last I can share with you the story of one serviceman's return from war with PTSD, and his inspiring journey back to his home and himself through the help of his steadfast service dog.

We all need the support and love of family—at no time more than Christmas. This is the story of one family who overcame obstacles to look deeper than the glitter and gaiety of the season to discover the true meaning of Christmas.

A Lowcountry Christmas

I will honour Christmas in my heart, and try to keep it all the year. I will live the Past, the Present, and the Future. The Spirits of all Three shall strive within me. I will not shut out the lessons that they teach!

—Scrooge, *A Christmas Carol,*
Charles Dickens

Prologue

CHRISTMAS EVE 2015

Taylor

It's Christmas Eve and for the first time in longer than I can remember, I'm happy. A cold wind rattles the shutters outdoors, but inside a gentle fire crackles in my hearth, even as one burns in my heart, warming me with serenity and peace.

Peace. I roll the word around in my mouth. It feels as fresh and new as the soft flakes of snow falling outside my window. And as rare. I live on Sullivan's Island, South Carolina, and I vividly remember the last time we saw snow. *Peace*. As a Marine who's seen more than my share of battles, it's a word I do not take lightly.

I didn't always feel joy at Christmas. In the first five years since I'd returned from Afghanistan, I've barely acknowledged the holiday. I have to smile now as I look around my living room—heavy boughs of pine and glossy magnolia leaves drape the mantel, the air thick with the scent of pine and burning wood. Across the room I see the two reasons for the joy in my heart—my wife and daughter. Harper, her face glowing with maternal love in the firelight, is sitting o

the sofa nursing Marietta. She's unaware that I'm standing across the room soaking in the sight, treasuring this moment, taking a mental photograph to keep forever. Many years from now when I'm old and my daughter is holding her own child, I'll pull this memory out from a dusty corner of my mind, smile, and think, *Ah, yes, that was Marietta's first Christmas.*

Though she's only three months old, seeing her fills me with dreams of Christmases still to come. Sitting in a wing chair by the fire, Mamaw, Marietta's great-grandmother and namesake, pauses from her knitting to sip her rum drink. I watch as her gaze drifts over to the baby and her face eases into a soft grin of winsome pleasure. I wonder what memories the old woman is pulling from the treasure trove in her mind as she gazes on the child. More than eighty Christmases . . .

I wonder, too, if memories aren't a part of the magic of Christmas. Not the shiny, new excitement of children. Rather, the muted memories that stir during this season to bring alive Christmases past—the smiles of departed loved ones, the voice-less carols sung in our hearts, and the exclamations of welcome, joy, and love. These treasured memories—captured moments from times long gone—envelop us in that matchless spirit of Christmas one season after the other, year after year, until we ourselves fade

and become part of the memories. I stare at my daughter and know that through her, I will live on.

I have journeyed the hard path of Scrooge to reach this insight. My heart was once so cold it chilled every room I entered. No smile could soften me. My face was so foreboding people didn't approach and children crossed the street when I approached. Christmas was just another day to endure. The New Year wasn't something to be anticipated, but rather something to dread. I confess, some fearsome nights I didn't want to see the dawn break the darkness.

These memories still have the power to chill me. I can feel their weight settle in my heart. I shake my head to free myself from their icy grip.

My dog, Thor, raises his head, and then climbs from his place by the fire to stand by me. He nudges my thigh with his nose. I look down to see his dark eyes watching me, so intently that I stop thinking and focus on him. Thor is my service dog, attuned to my every mood. Even while he was resting, he was monitoring my breathing, my body language. He sensed the anxiety that swept over me. I have PTSD and Thor knows all the danger signals, and how to deflect me before I slip into the abyss. I smile reassuringly and lay my hand on his broad head, finding comfort in his closeness. Thor is not a dog to be ignored. Part Great Dane and part Labrador, he's a whopping 120 pounds of devotion. *I'm okay,* I tell him with my eyes. Comprehending, Thor sits at my feet.

I stroke Thor's head as he leans against me and register the change in the music. Now Frank Sinatra is singing "I'll Be Home for Christmas," a song that always tugs at my heart and sends my mind drifting back to my Christmas homecoming five years ago. I let my gaze travel to the imposing eight-foot white fir tree dominating the far corner of the room. It stands tall and proud, as I do looking at it. I cut down this tree myself, drove it home strapped to the roof of my car as proud as any hunter would be of his trophy elk, and I basked in Harper's praises when she saw it. It's a looker, for sure. Harper claims I've set a high standard for every year to come. That's okay. I'm up to the challenge. Not because I'm six feet two inches tall and have the power to chop down a tree twice my size. But because I know in my heart I will track down one special tree and cut it down every year that I'm able to swing an ax in honor of that one tree that miraculous Christmas. It was a small, spindly tree, but it had the heart of a redwood.

It was the Christmas tree that changed everything.

Men's courses will foreshadow certain ends, to which, if persevered in, they must lead. But if the courses be departed from, the ends will change.

—Scrooge, *A Christmas Carol*

Chapter 1

WASHINGTON, DC
NOVEMBER 30, 2010

Taylor

I'm going home for Christmas. Back to McClellanville and the ocean. Back to my family.

I'm proud to be the son of a shrimper. While some men look at wide-open fields and think of planting, we McClellans stare out at the water and think of shrimp. Shrimping is hard work—long hours laboring under a relentless sun, straining muscles against nets dragged from the sea bulging with shrimp. My hands bear scars from years of separating shrimp from bycatch. Backbreaking work . . . and exhilarating. It's in our blood. Out on the water we're saltwater cowboys, untamed, unbridled, and free. Mavericks riding the water. I'm proud to bear the McClellan name. For as long as I can remember, my father, Alistair—everyone calls him the Captain—has steered the *Miss Jenny,* named after my mother, the largest shrimp boat in the fleet. I worked on the *Miss Jenny* as soon as I could walk. That's the way it is in the business—family pitches in.

I'm proud to wear the ring. I graduated from the

Citadel in Charleston, the first man in my family to graduate from college. It's a rare sight to see one's father so proud his eyes tear up. Especially a sea-hardened man such as the Captain. I'll never forget it.

I'm proud to be a Marine. I'm the son of a sailor and the most recent in a long line of men who've served their country in foreign wars. After graduating I immediately entered the Corps as an officer. "Dare to Lead" the Citadel challenged us, and that's what I did. After training I shipped off to the Middle East to lead a platoon. Our mission was to maintain a defensive perimeter in Afghanistan. We patrolled a vast area of desert, seeking out contraband and insurgents, racing across burning sand in hot pursuit of smugglers with small caches of weapons and ordnance. Small villages yielded the same.

You might not believe me, but the desert and the ocean are similar. They're both immense in a way that defies comprehension. I've ridden in a Humvee across miles of endless sand under a merciless sun and sailed a shrimp boat on the dark sea when the dawn broke across the horizon, and in both places I *felt* the vastness. It made me feel small and insignificant. Isolated and alone. Both desert and sea are unforgiving terrain and don't tolerate fools.

I'm proud that I'm a good leader. I don't say that with conceit. I say this so you understand why

I feel the burden of guilt for being sent home while some of my men will never make it back.

The Bible says that pride goeth before a fall. I'm here to tell you that's true.

Thanksgiving is over and the Christmas season is beginning. Instead of joy, however, I feel the terror of my war memories lurking inside my brain like one of those damned IEDs just waiting for the right trigger to explode and tear me apart, the way one did on a dusty Afghanistan road. The bomb shattered my bones and burned my body and soul. Yet they call me lucky.

I'm going home because the doctors say I'm recovered. I can only shake my head and think, *What fools*. My fractured bones might be healed, but my brain certainly isn't. The scars in my mind are the wounds that cut the deepest. I didn't want to leave the hospital—I felt safe there. I'm more comfortable with other injured servicemen like me than I am with my family. But they said I had to leave, so I did. I got a cheap apartment near the hospital. I holed up, afraid to go out, to deal with the public. I grew isolated, lonely. The doctors told me to go see my family for the holidays. Where do you go but home when there's no place else to go? So, as the song says, I'll be home for Christmas.

I feel as if I'm heading for a fall.

"A merry Christmas, uncle! God save you!" cried a cheerful voice. It was the voice of Scrooge's nephew, who came upon him so quickly that this was the first intimation he had of his approach. "Bah!" said Scrooge. "Humbug!"

—*A Christmas Carol*

Chapter 2

McCLELLANVILLE, 2010

Miller

There's magic in Christmas. How else can you explain how excited everyone gets when December rolls around? Or the smile that pops on people's faces when they hear a favorite carol or see Christmas decorations in shop windows? I don't believe in Santa. I mean, I'm not a kid anymore. I'm ten. But I'm not ashamed to admit I still get excited about Christmas.

And I'm not the only one. As soon as Thanksgiving was over, before the smell of turkey had even left the kitchen, Bubba, Tom, Dill, and me started arguing about what was better to ask for for Christmas—an Xbox or a PlayStation. Personally, I'm on team PlayStation. But I'd be happy with either. All I've got now is my older brother Taylor's hand-me-down Xbox. He's been in Afghanistan and is letting me use it while he's away. Dad said he doesn't like those video games and I should play outdoors, but I know it's because they're expensive. Mama said those games cost the moon. Bubba's dad is some big shot at the power company. They live in one of the fancy new houses on Jeremy Creek. Not that I'm jealous. But, see, Bubba knows he can ask for either game and get it. The rest of us just kinda hope.

Well, not all of us. I don't even hope. My dad is captain of a shrimp boat. I guess I have to get used to saying *was*. Times have gotten tough for shrimpers. He held on as long as he could, but he couldn't fight the high costs of fuel and the low cost of imported shrimp any longer. So after Thanksgiving he docked the boat for good. We don't talk about it at home, but it's what we're all thinking about. What are we going to do now?

All Daddy's ever been is a shrimp boat captain. And his father before him—for generations. It's all I've ever wanted to be when I grow up. My name is Miller McDaniel McClellan. There's a lot of history in that name. I'm the son of a long line of fishermen going back to the founding of this here town we live in.

Daddy's a hard worker and real smart. He's good with his hands, knows his way around machines, and can fix anything. Sometimes he crews for another shrimp boat. But mostly he does construction jobs whenever and wherever he can. Mama's working hard, too, out cleaning houses. She tells me not to worry: "We'll get by." But I can tell by the way she pays for groceries with cash and counts the change carefully that money's tight. So I'm pretty sure I won't be getting a PlayStation or an Xbox this year. I expect I won't even ask for one.

Besides, there's something else I want. A whole lot more. I want a dog. And not just any dog—one puppy in particular. It's a long shot, but this year I think I have a chance. See what I mean about Christmas? It's a time you can hope.

After school, Dill and I got on our bikes and headed across town to his house. He's my best friend. His real name is Dillard, after his mama's family name, like mine is Miller, but I call him Dill. His daddy is a shrimp boat captain, too. We've both been working on a shrimp boat since the day we could walk the decks, and that gives us a special bond.

McClellanville's not like anywhere else. Sure, I'm partial because of my name, but it's true. Picture a small town that looks like it came out of an old movie, and that's it. Most of the houses are white wood with fancy porches, one prettier than the next. Then there's Mrs. Fraser's house, the big tumbledown redbrick that's hidden behind thick oak trees and shrubs taller than me. If you can see the porch, you'll see cats sitting every-where. We call her the cat lady because she's always feeding the wild cats.

Daddy says folks here don't like change, and it's a good thing because we pretty much live surrounded by the wild. My house is on Jeremy Creek. It looks like a river to me and it winds through acres of wetlands clear to the Atlantic Ocean. That's the path the shrimp boats take to the sea. On the other side of town is the Marion National Forest. Town is just a few blocks of shops on Pinckney Street—our main street—with the Art Center, and T. W. Graham & Co., the town's restaurant. It's been around forever and a day. The town is all spruced up for the holidays with shiny green holly and pine boughs and wreaths on the doors. As Dill and I rode our bikes through the streets after school, I coasted to check out the decorated windows.

"Come on!" Dill shouted impatiently.

He was far ahead, so I gripped my handlebars and pushed to catch up. Just remembering why we were going to his house gave me a burst of energy. We turned onto a hard-packed road bordered by huge oaks and longleaf pines that towered over us. I wouldn't want to live this far into the Marion National Forest. It's over 250,000 acres of woods, marsh, and wild things. It's famous because this is where the patriot Francis Marion hid out against the British army during the Revolutionary War. He was called the Swamp Fox. You might've heard of him. The forest is so thick and the marsh so murky the British could never find him. Or maybe they just didn't want to go in. I can understand that. Just last month a coyote ate one of Dill's cats. Yep, I'd rather live by the ocean than the forest.

Dill's house looks more like a big cabin, and it backs up right to the forest. You can barely see it in the dark. His family bought it after Hurricane Hugo destroyed their house in 1989, along with a lot of others. McClellanville was ground zero for the hurricane. Dill's mama told me a boat was in their yard where the house used to be! After the hurricane his mother said she wouldn't live near the ocean. They didn't go too far. But here, deep in the forest, it feels miles from the water.

I dropped my bike on the ground and followed Dill into his house. A gruff bark of warning came from the back of the house, and a minute later Daisy, his chocolate-brown Lab, came trotting up to investigate. She passed by Dill and came to sniff my legs while I petted her head. I knew it was her habit because she's superprotective now, but I could barely stand still since I was so excited to see her puppies! After a minute she wagged her tail and took the dog biscuit I always bring her. She'll let me pass into the back room now.

"Hi, boys," Mrs. Davidson called, sticking her head out from the kitchen. "How was school?"

"Good," we replied in monotone unison.

"I made some cookies."

I could smell the chocolate and my mouth watered, but nothing could keep me away from those puppies a second longer. "Thanks, Mrs. Davidson, but I'm not hungry. Can I see the puppies?"

Mrs. Davidson smiled the way mothers do when they aren't fooled. "Sure. Be gentle with them, hear? They're not so steady on their feet. But they're already getting into mischief."

Dill and I shot like bullets to the family room. I could hear the high-pitched yelping before I could see them. This is why I come to Dill's house every day after school. The brown leather furniture was pushed back to accommodate the large black wire enclosure that corralled seven brown and yellow balls of fur. The puppies came racing to the edge, excitedly climbing over each other, whimpering for our attention.

Seeing a bunch of puppies just does something to your heart. Never fails. I couldn't stop the "Awwww" that came from my mouth. I'd have been embarrassed but Dill was doing the same thing. I stepped over the railing, and suddenly was surrounded, each puppy trying to lick my nose, my ears. I was enveloped in a cloud of puppy breath. I laughed out loud, not only because it tickled but because they were so darn cute. I loved all seven of them. But I had eyes for only one.

I singled out one golden puppy and settled him in my lap. This one is mine. I called him Sandy Claws because he likes to dig. But also because it was Christmas. I came to Dill's right after the puppies were born, so I knew them as well as anyone. For weeks, when Dill's mother went to work in the afternoon, Dill and I babysat the pups. We did our homework sitting outside the fenced puppy arena. When they were newborns, they slept a lot. Now, not so much.

Dill's mother came into the room with a plate of cookies. "It's uncommon how that puppy really takes to you."

"He chose me," I said with pride. "He comes straight to my side and just stays here. Falls asleep right in my lap." Sandy looked up at me, then stretched higher to lick my nose.

Mrs. Davidson set the plate on the side table and clasped her hands. She turned to face me, and she looked worried. "Miller, the puppies will be ready to go by Christmas. See all the colored ribbons?"

I noticed that most of the puppies now had ribbons tied around their necks in all different colors. I nodded, even as I saw that Sandy wasn't wearing one.

"Those puppies have already sold. And I have a list of people who want one. I'm letting them come by this week to see the puppies and make a choice." She paused. "Miller, one couple especially likes Sandy. I've tried to tell people he's taken but . . . Well, he's a very handsome boy. I can't hold on to him much longer."

My grip tightened around my puppy. No one could have Sandy but me.

"Honey, did you talk to your mama yet about whether you can get him?"

Sandy began to squirm in my tight grip. I loosened my arms but was unwilling to let him go. He stared up at me as though he could feel my tension. "Not yet. I, uh, I was thinking I could ask for him for Christmas."

Mrs. Davidson's face softened with worry. "I know, honey, Dill told me. I wish I could wait, but, you see, people want to buy the pups for Christmas gifts. They need to know now. And so do I."

My lips tightened and my heart began pounding faster. The pups cost $300 each. That was as much as a video-game box.

"I was wondering, just in case," I hedged. "I have seventy-five dollars saved. Could I give that to you as a deposit and just keep paying you bit by bit till I'm all paid up? I'll work really hard. I promise."

She smiled, but it was a sad smile. "You mean you want to buy him on layaway?"

I glanced at Dill. He was looking at the brown puppy in his lap, petting it with his face scrunched up with worry. His brown puppy had a red ribbon around its neck because Dill was getting to keep that puppy for himself for Christmas. I reckon he was embarrassed about not being able to just give me one.

I shrugged, not knowing what *layaway* meant. "I guess."

Mrs. Davidson sighed, then walked closer to

crouch down to me. She was being kind, but I knew bad news was coming.

"Honey, I wish I could say yes. But I can't and here's why. Buying the puppy is the cheapest part. You have to have money to take the dog to the vet, buy food and flea meds, and a whole lot more. It totals up to a lot of money. It wouldn't be right for me to let you buy this puppy without your parents' permission. They'll have to own the dog with you. Do you understand? I wish I could, but I love the puppy too much to take that risk. And I'm too good of friends with your mama not to have her consent." She paused. "Tell you what. You can have this puppy—and by the way, I think he's the pick of the litter—for two hundred dollars. That will help some, I hope. Miller, do you want me to talk to your mother for you?"

I shook my head, eyes cast down on the pup. I didn't want her to see the tears welling up. I knew if she called my mama, she'd give Mrs. Davidson all the reasons we couldn't have a dog. I needed to plead my case with my mother first.

"No, thank you, ma'am. I'll talk to her tonight." I looked up and met her gaze. "I promise."

She reached out to pat my head. It made me feel like one of the puppies.

"I hope she says yes. I know that puppy loves you."

• • •

I rode my bike home as fast as I could. A cold front was setting in, and my fingers felt frozen on my handlebars. The air was moist and chilled, like snow. Not that I've ever seen snow. But the thought of snow gave me hope. My mama told me about the snow that fell on Christmas after Hurricane Hugo. She said it seemed to McClellanville as though God was sending them his blessing after the devastation of the storm.

Daylight was dimming by the time I got home. My house is not as fancy as the Victorian houses on Pinckney Street, nor as big as Dill's house, but it's a right pretty house with a broad front porch and gabled windows. They look like a smile when I come home. Best of all, the house sits right on Jeremy Creek, a stone's throw from the shrimp boat docks. Like a lot of houses, it could use some TLC. "Fixing houses takes money," my mother always says with a sorry shake of her head when she studies the peeling paint or steps on a wobbly stair. But it's home and we don't ever plan to leave.

Inside the house it was warm and smelled of baking bread. I followed my nose to the kitchen, with its row of windows overlooking the creek. Mama was bent over the long wood-block table putting the top doughy crust onto a potpie. Beside it was the carcass of the old Thanksgiving turkey, cleaned practically to the bone. Mama doesn't believe in serving a puny turkey on Thanksgiving. As much as I love turkey, and while it makes a nice break from shrimp, we've been eating leftovers ever since. I'm hoping this is her last-ditch effort to strip every lick of meat from the bones into her potpie. I sigh, knowing she'll use the bones for soup.

Mama's a lean, tidy woman. She's real pretty. Especially her hair. It's long and dark brown, though she's not happy about the white that winds through it now. Daddy calls them silver threads, and she always smiles when he does. She's got it pulled back now, though some strands are falling down along her neck. Her white baker's apron is dusty with flour. She's lost some weight in the past few months. She's a substitute teacher but since Daddy stopped shrimping she's started cleaning houses for extra money. Her dress hangs shapelessly from her shoulders, and her face looks tired. But when she looked up to see me, her green eyes sparkled with pleasure and her smile changed her face to look young again.

"You're back!" Automatically she glanced up at the clock. "I was beginning to worry."

I went to the table and slid into a chair. I was tired after the long bike ride. "Sorry I'm late."

"Did you get your homework done at Dill's?"

I shook my head. I thought about lying, but the

one thing Mama hates more than anything is lying. "Family doesn't lie to one another," she's told me every time she's found me out. I didn't want to get on her bad side today. "No."

She stilled and glanced at me. "How much homework do you have?"

To my relief she didn't scold. I slipped off my backpack and dug into it, pulling out a book. I laid it on the table with resignation. "Not much. We have to start reading this for a book report."

Mama wiped her hands on her apron and reached for the book. Her eyes lit up with pleasure. "Oh, *A Christmas Carol*! I love this book. It's great."

"I seen the movie already." I groaned softly.

"Saw," she corrected. "The movie is good, but the book is better. No one can describe people better than Charles Dickens. Have you read any of it?"

I shook my head. "I just got it today."

"You've heard of Scrooge, haven't you? The grouchy old skinflint who hated Christmas? He said, 'Bah, humbug,' whenever anyone wished him joy of the season."

"What's a humbug?"

Mama laughed, a light cheery sound. "*You're* a humbug," she said jokingly, tousling my hair. "No, it means 'nonsense.' Or 'deception.' "

I smirked and moved my head from under her

hand. "The high school is doing the play and we all have to go see it."

"Really? Oh, wonderful!" Her smile widened. "We'll make it a special night."

I shrugged, uncaring. I didn't want to go.

"Don't be an old Scrooge." Mama laughed again and went back to her potpie. She added jovially, "It's Christmastime!"

I brightened at hearing this. That was her rallying call, and it being December 1, she was right on schedule. I don't know anyone who loves Christmas more than my mama. Or any holiday, for that matter. Daddy says she's a fool for holidays, but he always smiles when he says it. If Mama is thinking about Christmas, I figure it's a good time to ask about the puppy.

"You remember I told you about Dill's dog, Daisy, having puppies?"

Mama's hand stilled a moment on the pie. "Uh-huh."

"They're real cute. Mrs. Davidson says they're Daisy's best litter ever. And healthy!" I was laying it on thick. "She already took them to the vet and got them shots. They don't have worms, neither," I added for good measure.

"That's good." Mama shifted her gaze and returned to working on her pie.

"Yeah." I nodded. My mind was spinning. *How should I ask? Should I be direct or clever? Kind of weave it into a conversation?* I went for the latter. “A lot of the guys are asking for Xboxes or PlayStations this Christmas.”

“That’s a pretty big ask.”

“Yeah, but I think they’ll get one.”

“Really?” She looked up, finished with her pie. She wiped her hands again on her apron. I noticed how red they’ve become. “Is that what you want for Christmas?”

I tried to act casual. I lifted a shoulder. “I wouldn’t mind one.” I glanced her way. “But it’s not what I want.”

Mama turned and checked the oven. She was efficient in the kitchen, moving from place to place with the sure-footedness of an NBA player. She paused, then looked up at me, giving me her full attention. “What *do* you want for Christmas?”

Here it comes, I thought. Leaning forward on the table the words rushed out: “Oh, Mama, one of the puppies is the best dog I’ve ever seen. He’s a golden color, and he’s a real sweet dog. I call him Sandy Claws, get it?” I laughed nervously. She smiled but her eyes were sad. “And he likes me already. He always comes and lies right next to me. And he sleeps in my lap and everything! I love him, Mama. He’s the only thing I want for Christmas. I’ll take care of him and walk him and I’ll get a part-time job so I can help pay for his food.” My words were gushing from my mouth so fast I had to stop and take a breath. I looked at her and ended my outburst with my hands pressed together in prayer. "Please?" My whole body strained forward.

Mama looked at me and I could see a sorrow that went deep in her eyes. She didn't speak, and I felt my body slowly release its tension as I slid back in the chair, like a deflated balloon. I could see what her answer was before she spoke the words. I could see that she'd already talked to Mrs. Davidson.

"Oh, honey. It's not a good time to get a dog."

The disappointment washed over me like a wave. I scowled, hurt and angry. "It's never a good time."

"That's not fair."

"You're right! It isn't fair!" I shot back at her, surprised by my own boldness. "You always say I'm too young or that dogs are too dirty or that maybe when the right dog comes along, or when I'm older. Well, I'm older now and this *is* the right dog. I love him, Mama." I felt tears moisten my eyes and was embarrassed.

Mama sighed and her shoulders slumped. "You know things are tight since your daddy put the boat to dock. I don't know . . ." She took a deep breath and said as a final excuse, "I suppose we could ask your father."

"Ask me what?"

We both spun around. We'd been so intent on our discussion that neither of us had heard him come in. Daddy filled the threshold, his broad shoulders straining his worn jean jacket. His clothes were soiled with dirt and oil that spoke of a hard day's work on a shrimp boat. His face was deeply tanned year-round and coursed with lines like the creeks he navigated. His pale eyes shone out in contrast like beacons that telegraphed intensity. The light shone on my mother, then on me.

The look in his eyes made me sit straighter in my chair. I couldn't speak and turned and looked helplessly at my mother.

She was flustered by his surprise entrance and hurried to his side to offer him a quick kiss. "You're home early."

"The catch was lousy," he said with a disappointed grunt.

"Want a beer?" Without waiting for a reply Mama hurried to the fridge to fetch him one.

Daddy opened the bottle and took a long drink. Then he fixed his gaze on me. "Ask me what?"

Mama came to my rescue. "Miller was just telling me what he wanted for Christmas."

A shadow crossed Daddy's face. He took another swig from his beer. "So what do you want?"

I licked my lips and rose to stand. "A puppy. One of Dill's puppies."

He didn't speak.

I rushed on. "He's a golden Lab. Pick of the litter, Mrs. Davidson says."

"A dog?" he asked with a shocked expression. "You want a *dog?*"

I nodded, mute.

"Hell, boy, do you know how much it costs to keep a dog?"

"I'd work to help pay for his food and stuff. You know I'm a good worker."

"You are that." He conceded and rubbed his stubbled jaw. He glanced at my mother, then shook his head. "But it won't be enough. Maybe next year."

"Not next year!" I cried. My desperation made me bold. "I don't want any dog, I want *this* dog! Sandy. I have to get him. *Please,* Daddy."

"Not now, Son. I can't afford to keep food on the table for you, much less a dog."

"I have seventy-five dollars. I'll give it all to you."

Color flooded my father's face. "I said *no,*" he shouted.

"Don't shout," Mama said.

"Don't encourage him!" he shot back at her, anger sparking.

A moment passed between them, a message signaled in their eyes that I didn't understand.

Daddy calmed and said, "Don't let him get his hopes up."

I could see I'd lost. I knew I should've been

quiet, but I couldn't stop myself. "I'd pay you back. Every penny. I swear."

"No!" he bellowed, and swiped his hand through the air like a machete cutting wheat. "No dog! That's the end of it, hear? Not another word." He glared at me a moment, but more hurt than anger was in his eyes. Then he stomped out of the room, leaving me and my mother standing in a stunned silence.

I slid back into my chair and rested my head in my arms, trying hard not to let the tears loose.

My mother came to my side and rested her palm on my shoulder. "Aw, Miller, don't feel bad. Daisy will have puppies again."

"Not like Sandy," I cried, my voice muffled by my arms.

"You don't know that. She always has beautiful pups. I know for a fact Mrs. Davidson is breeding her one more time."

She paused, waiting for me to say something. But I had nothing to say.

"Cheer up." She gently shook my shoulders. "I have some wonderful news. The best news."

I sniffed and raised my head. That's the thing about hope. You can beat it down and crush it, but it'll still bubble back up at the slightest chance. I wildly wondered if she'd heard of some job I could get, or that maybe she'd talked to Mrs. Davidson.

"Your brother is coming home!" Mama said

with heart. Her eyes shone with the news. "Can you believe it? Taylor coming home is our family's best Christmas present! Isn't that wonderful?"

That was the big news? I loved my big brother, and I was glad he was coming home. But that was my Christmas present? No Xbox. No PlayStation. And worst of all, no Sandy.

I wiped my eyes with my sleeve and stepped away from the table, away from her. I roughly grabbed my copy of *A Christmas Carol* and stuffed it back into my book bag with an angry shove. I felt hurt roiling inside me like a storm.

"Miller, don't be like that. It's Christmastime!"

Stomping away, I turned at the door and shouted with a voice that sounded like my father's, "Bah, humbug!"

There is nothing in the world so irresistibly contagious as laughter and good-humour.

—*A Christmas Carol*

Chapter 3
Jenny

A mother was only as happy as her most unhappy child.

I watched my son turn his back on me and stride from the kitchen, slinging his backpack over his shoulder. His every movement radiated anger and disappointment, and it hit me like a tidal wave.

Bah, humbug. Miller was a bright boy, and he knew that his quoting Scrooge, after my definition of the phrase, would deliver all the more impact. I tightened my lips, trying to still my careening emotions. Those were not sentiments a ten-year-old boy should feel at Christmas.

I brought my shaking fingertips to my lips and closed my eyes tight. A mother was the foundation of her family, I believed. It was up to me to create a home rich with traditions, values, and morals that would instill confidence in my children. At no time was this more true than at Christmas. Wasn't this the holiday that brought families together? A happy time meant for laughter, sentimental gifts, and love? And this holiday was extra special because Taylor was coming home from war. We had so much to be thankful for, so much to celebrate.

I sniffed and straightened my shoulders. This wasn't the time for weakness or tears. We were having tough times, sure, but love and laughter were not things that could be purchased—they came from the heart. It was up to me as the mother to make this holiday the happiest Christmas ever. I pulled the stray strands of hair from my face and tightened the elastic, wiped my hands on my apron, then determinedly walked to the turkey potpie resting on the table. My fingers began to move expertly around the crust, pinching the dough to tighten the seal. As I worked, I saw again Miller's face when his father had shouted no. *Pinch*. The crumpling of dreams, the wide eyes of sorrow filling with tears. *Pinch*. His head buried in his arms. *Pinch*. Finally his defiant anger and his rejection of Christmas.

My hands stilled, my head lowered, and my shoulders slumped with the weight of my son's unhappiness. I felt his crushing disappointment in my heart. I wanted to make his dream come true with the puppy. But I didn't have the money, and more, I wouldn't cross my husband on this. What could I do to make Miller feel better? I wondered. My anguish came from realizing nothing would. He'd see my efforts as nothing more than this turkey potpie, a desperate attempt to recycle tidbits from holidays past.

• • •

Three days passed and Miller was still giving us the cold shoulder. When I called out, "Good morning," Miller ignored me and sat sullenly at the kitchen table and shoved cereal in his mouth in silent protest. It was more of the same at dinner. I let him sulk, understanding he needed time to get over his disappointment. But when the weekend arrived and he was still acting this way, I decided enough was enough.

A December cold front had settled in the lowcountry. When I awoke, I peered out the bedroom window to see a coating of frost sparkling on the tips of the grass. A knowing smile crossed my lips. My grandmother once told me the best time to gather from the woods was after a frost had killed off the bugs. Old wives' tale, perhaps, but it signaled it was time for the Christmas Forage.

Even though it was Saturday, Alistair had risen and left before dawn to spend the day out on a shrimp boat. The season would soon end, and I worried he'd take a job on a boat in Florida. That would mean months away from home. I'd heard the tales of women whose husbands followed the shrimp south, of the floozies who hung around the bars the way laughing gulls did docks, and the drinks that led to bad choices. Many marriages ended after a few of the rowdier trips, and I didn't want to be another statistic. But he was hell-bent on earning money for his family, and there was no stopping the Captain when his mind was made up. I had seen the shame in his eyes when he'd told his son he couldn't afford a dog. He'd always been a proud man, the best captain in these parts. The disgrace of docking his boat was coming down hard on him and could make him mean. I was walking a thin line between support and frustration.

I dressed quickly in jeans and a thick sweater. As I walked down the hall toward the stairs, I paused at Taylor's room. Pushing open the door, I couldn't help but peer inside. The scent of pine soap permeated the room, fresh and clean. I'd spent most of yesterday afternoon freshening it up for his arrival. The small navy-and-white room was just as he'd left it four years earlier when he'd entered the Marines. The Corps insignia hung on the wall beside that of the Citadel. I leaned against the doorframe and allowed myself the luxury of wandering back in my memories to when Taylor was a small boy. How many times had I tucked him into bed in this room? Taylor had been our only child for most of his childhood. He could do no wrong in my eyes and he rarely disappointed me. His father doted on him, too—despite their rows. The problem was they were too much alike. Taylor had Alistair's good qualities—he was fair-minded, honest, hardworking, a natural leader, and deeply kind. They were both big men, broad shouldered and square jawed. Taylor also shared some of his father's not-so-good traits. They could be stubborn and opinionated. Also like Alistair, Taylor was a man of few words, but when he spoke, his words were well thought out and people listened.

I let my fingertips glide over the bedpost and the navy coverlet, and smiled, remembering how at bedtime a young Taylor would sometimes ask for "a chat with the light out." Those were golden moments. Taylor didn't share his feelings readily, yet somehow the darkness allowed him to open up. He'd lie on his back, hands under his head, and tell me about his day, just rambling on about this or that. I'd listen, capturing each word. It was music to my ears.

I sighed, bringing my hand to my cheek. Taylor was twenty-six now and hadn't shared anything personal with me in a long time. I hadn't even seen him in over a year. I felt his absence deeply. It was almost five months since he'd arrived back in the States. I'd wanted to fly to Andrews Air Force Base to greet him when he got off the plane. But he'd been firm when he'd told me not to come. Money being tight, I'd agreed, but it still niggled at me. I could have surprised him. The thought that my son had arrived back on American soil injured and alone still hurt. But I was careful never to complain. Every day I thanked God that my baby had come home alive.

And he'd be home in a few more days, I reminded myself, pushing off from the wall. I was going to spoil him rotten! I'd start by giving him the welcome home he deserved. Oh, what a party I'd planned! Wouldn't he be surprised? I smiled and crossed the room, eager to get my day rolling.

Next I passed Miller's room. I slowly pushed open the door for a peek inside. The door creaked softly and I cringed, not wanting to wake him. Shafts of light from the blinds illuminated the boy sleeping on the twin bed. He was on his belly, twisted in his blue-and-white duvet covered with sailing ships. He wanted his room to be the same color as his adored older brother's.

Miller had been my surprise child. Like Sarah in the Bible I'd born a son later in life, and he had been my and Alistair's blessing. Miller was more like me than Alistair and Taylor. He had always been my helper, at my side, watching, observing, readily absorbing anything I taught him. When he grew older, Miller, unlike Taylor, didn't hold back on his feelings or the gossip from school. He didn't need the lights out to share his thoughts. Miller talked openly night and day.

Which was why his silence now was so disturbing. I missed my chatterbox. I slowly closed the door again. Today, my focus was on

Miller. His heart was broken and he needed my help to get past his anger.

Making my way downstairs, I let my gaze wander the rooms, assessing what needed to be done that day. It was an old house. It had once belonged to a McClellan, another shrimp boat captain, but over the years it had been sold. It was a great day in the Captain's life when he bought the house and brought it back into family hands. I loved the house even more than he did. The trawler, the *Miss Jenny*, was Alistair's terrain. This house with all its wood-paneled rooms and beams, the dentil molding, built-in shelves, was my domain. The navy sofa was lumpy, the plaid fabrics on the wing chairs were frayed, the cane seat of the old rocker by the fire needed recaning, but put them all together and they made a cozy room in the early-morning light. The house was neither large nor grand. But it had history . . . and it was mine.

Clothes lay strewn about on the furniture, dishes were left in front of the television, dying flowers drooped on the table. Entering the kitchen, I paused. Best of all, every morning I could come into this kitchen and greet the day while staring out at my beloved Jeremy Creek. The sight never failed to take my breath away. This time of year the wide creek curved through the vast acres of gold and brown cordgrass like a snake, stretching far out to the Intracoastal and the ocean beyond. I loved this old house, one of the oldest in an old town dating back to 1861. None of the bigger, newer houses along the creek with all their bells and whistles made me wish for more. I had what money couldn't buy—craftsmanship from a day gone by. Besides, I wasn't the fancy type. Flannel and denim suited me more than silk and cashmere. And today, boots! It was time for the Christmas Forage!

I reached for my heavy iron skillet from its place of honor over the stove. This treasured heirloom had been passed down from mother to daughter for generations. I'd make a hearty breakfast for Miller. I smiled smugly to myself as I pulled a thick slab of bacon from the fridge. Nothing could lure a boy from his bed faster than the scent of bacon sizzling on the stove.

For it is good to be children sometimes, and never better than at Christmas, when its mighty Founder was a child Himself.

—*A Christmas Carol*

Chapter 4
Miller

Do I smell bacon? Who can ignore that? I pushed back my covers and went downstairs, sniffing like a hound on the scent. Mama was standing at the big iron stove, humming as she flipped sizzling bacon in the cast-iron pan. She turned and smiled when I walked in.

"Morning, sleepyhead. There's a stack of pancakes on the table, help yourself. Bacon will be up in a minute."

I slid into a chair and grabbed the pitcher of warm maple syrup. After drenching the pancakes, I dug in. I'd already eaten two when Mama put several pieces of crisp bacon on my plate. She stood beside me and watched as I hungrily devoured a piece.

"Eat up," she said with gusto as she turned back to the stove. "We have a busy day ahead of us."

"Huh?" I swung my head to look at her.

Mama's eyes gleamed as she picked up her coffee cup. "It's time for our Christmas Forage!"

The Christmas Forage was an outing that we went on every year. Our mission was to collect pine and fir branches, holly, pinecones, and whatever other decorations caught our eyes in the woods. It was special. Just the two of us. No one else came along. She called me her Christmas helper, but I always teased back that I was really her slave.

I looked up at her smiling face, and her eyes were bright with hope. She knew I was still mad at her and Daddy, that my heart was still aching about the dog. But I knew she felt bad about it and was trying to make me feel better. I wanted to stay mad, but this was our special time. And when I saw that hope in her eyes, I just couldn't hurt her. I loved her too much.

So I caved. Brusquely, I nodded and went back to my breakfast. I had to save face, after all.

With every step, I heard a crunch in the thick forest floor of leaves. The air was crisp and laden with the musky scent of autumn. In South Carolina the winters come slow. Not till December do the icy winds and frosts hit us, unlike in Chicago where my uncle lives. There are already inches of snow on the ground. Or even in the mountains of North Carolina, where the roads are already slick with ice. People from off always yammer on about how the seasons never change here. They're used to looking up into the trees to see the colors go from green to yellow, orange, then red. They just don't know where to look when they're in our neck of the woods. Mama says that the most magical changes of season occur in the wetlands, where the grass turns gold in the fall, then brown in the winter, then come spring you see the bright green stalks peeking out at the base of all the brown grass, until summer, when the vast expanse is a wonder of waving green dotted with white egrets. We look up and see the migrating birds that stream along our coast on their long journey south in the winter, then back north in the spring. Every fall Mama and I get our binoculars and make a list of all the migrating birds we spot. Yes, sir, here along the coast the change of seasons is a living, breathing miracle.

We walked a few paces, Mama's stride slow, her head turning with careful scrutiny of the forest floor and leafy canopy. She's spry like I imagine a woodland fairy to be. When she strolls, her dark hair fans out behind her and her eyes gleam with the joy of the hunt. It's like being deep in the forest frees her somehow. With each step deeper into the woods the creases and lines of worry leave her eyes and a soft smile rests on her face.

I followed behind her, pulling the rusty, trusty red Radio Flyer wagon that used to be mine when I was a kid. It was a good toy then, but it's a good tool now. We use it to lug all the loot we gather from our forage trips to the woods, the beach, the docks. We'd been out to the forest earlier in the fall to collect pounds of pecans for her Thanks-giving pecan pies. Mama calls it "going nutting." She knows a secret spot where the best pecan trees dwell. She won't tell anyone where it is, save for me.

"Sworn to secrecy," she told me. "My mama told me, and her mama told her. The pecans from those trees are always the sweetest and most buttery. Good genes. Like us."

We laughed then as we always did when she told me this story. And she told it every year. We gathered the nuts in cloth sacks and stored them in a cool, dry place. Even after all her Thanksgiving pies we still have plenty left for Christmas. Mama doesn't hunt for nuts now. This late in the year the squirrels have beaten us to anything worth eating. I'm glad because it's backbreaking work, stooping over to pick out the nuts from the leaves under the trees. We collected black walnuts, too. They're hard to open. After we lugged them home, Mama and I spread them out in the gravel driveway and she drove her car over them to break the husks. Sometimes she even lets me drive.

For the Christmas Forage, Mama searched for branches of cedar, fir, and longleaf pine. The sound of her clippers clicking away was like the sound the pileated woodpeckers make. She handed the clippings to me to put in the baskets—magnolia leaves, holly berries, pinecones. When our baskets were full to the brim, the scent of pine was so strong I could almost taste it.

Gathering Spanish moss was Mama's job. She wore thick gloves and put on a yellow slicker while harvesting because so many bugs were hiding in the moss—the worst of all were the chiggers. She stretched far up with a bow rake to pull the Spanish moss from the trees, then put it directly into black plastic bags. When she was done, she shook herself off like a dog and stripped off her gloves and slicker.

"Someday you're going to be old enough for this job."

"Someday." I smirked. "But not today."

When we headed back home, we took turns pulling the wagon. The walking and the work made us hungry for more than the snacks Mama had packed us. But we basked in the glow of our success.

"This might be our best haul ever," Mama said, looking over the baskets that overflowed with boughs and berries.

She says that every year, too. I ventured a smile.

Mama was quick to catch it. "Feeling better?"

"I guess."

"Being outdoors always makes a body feel better." She walked a few feet, her heels crunching in the composted earth. "I'm glad. You know, I'm sad when you're sad."

"I didn't just feel sad," I complained, not wanting her to diminish my pain. "Mama, my heart actually *hurt.* It still does."

"I know," she said, more softly now. "And I'm sorry."

We walked awhile in silence.

"You know, your daddy felt real bad that he had to say no to the puppy."

I snorted. "He didn't sound sad. He sounded mad." I grimaced, feeling a spurt of my anger return. "He's always mad."

"That's because he's feeling so bad about putting the *Miss Jenny* up to dock. Working that boat wasn't just his job, it was his way of life."

I stopped short and turned to face her. "But, see, that's what I don't get. Why'd he do it? Daddy was the best shrimper around—everybody said so. How come he had to put his boat up and others don't?"

"A lot of others did."

"Not Dill's dad." There. It was what I'd wanted to say for a long time.

Mama puffed out a breath. "No, not Dill's dad. Captain Davidson is hanging on, but he's got a smaller boat." She looked at me with intent so I'd understand. "The *Miss Jenny* is one of the bigger boats on the docks, so it costs more to run. You know your daddy hung on as long as he could. But the simple truth is he couldn't afford to keep the boat on the water any longer. The price of diesel fuel has shot sky-high and the cost of imported shrimp has fallen so low—that's a bad combination for the local shrimp. Plus," she said enviously, "Brenda Davidson has a right fine job that pays well so she can help keep things afloat."

"You have a good job."

Mama smirked. "Well, I have a job."

"Are we really broke?"

Mama expelled a short laugh of surprise. But her smile fell when she saw that I wanted an honest answer.

"I'm not a baby anymore. You can tell me."

Mama sighed and reached out to take hold of the wagon's handle. She gave it a yank and continued walking, her face lost in thought. "Things are tight," she said, looking down at her boots while she walked. "Not that you have to worry. We're getting by. We have a roof over our heads and food on the table. But," she added with emphasis, "we don't have anything left over for extras."

Like a dog, I thought to myself.

I remembered how I saw her cutting up her credit cards, how my daddy went out every morning looking for work, and how every evening he sat at his desk late at night, his chin in his palm, looking over the bills.

"So I'm really not getting Sandy." I knew the answer but just had to ask.

"No, honey. Not this year." She forced a smile. "But there's always next year. Or maybe even this summer."

"Sure."

Mama stopped, dropped the wagon handle, and turned to put her hands on my shoulders. She lowered so we looked eye to eye. "I promise you, Miller, I'll get you a dog, hear? As soon as Daddy finds full-time work."

I nodded okay. It was only polite, knowing she was sincere. But I felt all the worse because whatever dog came down the pike, it wouldn't be Sandy.

We walked a bit longer, and with each step it felt like my hope for Sandy was disappearing in this big ol' empty hole in my heart.

"Miller?" Mama said in a quiet voice.

"Yeah . . . ?"

"Do you believe in Santa Claus?"

"What?" I swung my head around. "Me? Mama, I'm ten," I told her with a hint of disgust.

Mama tried to hide her smile. "Of course. . . . Well, do you believe in Christmas miracles?"

My heart skipped as hope seeped in. "Do you?"

Mama paused, then swung her head to look at me and nodded. "I do," she replied emphatically. "I really do. Take your brother. I prayed and prayed that he'd come home to me, and there he was, in this horrible explosion. Some of his comrades were killed, but he lived. And now he's coming home for Christmas." She lifted one arm as though to say, *See what I mean?* "If that's not a Christmas miracle, I don't know what is."

I wasn't convinced. "Mama, I'll tell you what my idea of a Christmas miracle is. If I wake up on Christmas morning and find Sandy under the tree, not only will I believe in miracles, but I'll believe in Santa Claus!"

Mama stopped short and bent over with a guffaw that rang through the trees. When she straightened, her face was lit with laughter. She moved closer to bump me with her hip. "Well, all right then. If that happens, we'll both get our Christmas miracles." She added with more sincerity, "I hope yours comes true, Miller. I really, truly do."

I didn't know what to think then. Was she going to get me a dog as a surprise? Or was she just trying to get my spirits up again? This Christmas wishing was wearing me out.

Mama bent to pick up the wagon handle and began walking again. "Yes, sir, it's our best haul yet," she said in that cheery voice meant to change the subject. "And I couldn't have done it without my best helper. Aren't we the smart ones? We don't need to spend a penny for the best decorations in town." Mama's grin mixed pleasure with pride.

I didn't respond, lost in my thoughts about whether I might get a dog.

Suddenly Mama burst out singing, "Have a holly, jolly Christmas." She looked at me expectantly, cuing me for the next line.

It was our favorite carol, the one we began our rounds of Christmas carols with every year. Of course I joined in: ". . . It's the best time of the year."

We sang carols as we walked the narrow path back to the truck, favorites that we knew the words to, sometimes taking turns with harmony.

When we got home, Mama set right to work. One by one she shook out all the boughs, trimmed the ends of the branches, and stuck them in big plastic pails of water out on the porch.

"Now comes the grisly part," she said, slipping on a thick pair of garden gloves. "We have to kill off any creepy crawlies that decided to hitch a ride."

She put back on her slicker and began pulling apart the long strands of Spanish moss like cotton candy and spread it out on the front walkway. Crouching low, she picked out twigs, leaves, and insects stubbornly clinging to the strands. Now came the hard part. Together we set up a huge pot that Daddy used to boil crabs. She filled it with water, added dish detergent, then swished the moss strands like we were washing clothes by hand, picking out bits of debris. With clump after clump she repeated this, then rinsed them with the hose. Next I cleaned the pot and filled it with fresh water.

"My mama used to check the moss for bugs, then put it up, but I don't take that chance. I don't want bugs in my clean house." She set her chin. "I cook 'em up."

And that's what she did. She boiled the moss in small batches for a few minutes, then after it cooled I helped her hang the moss on a drying rack made of an old wood ladder and two sawhorses. She let me help now that the chiggers were dead. Side by side we bent over the moss, picking out the last bits of twigs or dead insects.

When we were done, our backs were aching and I was fit to eat a horse.

"What seemed like a windfall was really a whole lot of work," I complained.

"There's more satisfaction in decorating the house with things we made ourselves." Mama crossed her arms and looked at the hanging moss. The sky was darkening and a hush had settled over the landscape. Mama's face was a silhouette in the shadows. "Someday we'll look back on today, Miller, and think all this work was the best part of Christmas. Going out to forage for treasures. You and me, on our great holiday adventure."

"After our backs are healed."

She laughed. "Agreed. Now come on, partner. We're not done yet."

By the time it got dark outside, the kitchen was

covered with baked pinecones, smilax, berries, greens, garden wire, wreath frames, and all manner of craft supplies. When Daddy walked in at six, he was carrying a pizza.

"Hope you like pepperoni," he called out.

Having pizza on the night Mama does her decorations is a tradition in our family. Daddy lit a roaring fire, the first of the winter, and we gathered around the coffee table in the living room, sitting on the floor to eat our pizza like on a camping trip. As I lazily chewed the warm cheesy crust, I looked over at my mama and daddy and I saw that they were smiling and talking in low voices like in the days before the boat was docked. I smiled then, too, thinking that maybe it would be an all-right Christmas after all.

I'm too old and beyond hope! Go and redeem some younger, more promising creature, and leave me to keep Christmas in my own way!

—Scrooge, *A Christmas Carol*

Chapter 5
Jenny

The phone was ringing off the hook all day, and all the calls were either for Taylor or the surprise homecoming party we were throwing for him. My emotions were soaring—the excitement, the anticipation, the joy—it was like old times when Taylor lived at home. With his all-American good looks and good nature, he was always popular with guys and girls alike. Everyone was excited he was coming home and wanted to be waiting for him with open arms. No one more than me.

"Taylor's homecoming is our best Christmas present!" I kept telling everyone, meaning it. Because it was a gift that my son was returning home from the war—safe and sound—during the holiday. My family deserved this perfect Christmas gift. Something to celebrate.

It had been a long roller coaster of a year. Even before Taylor's deployment I'd felt his absence. When Taylor left for the Marines, everything seemed to change. It seemed he took the youth and vivacity of the house with him. When he was at home, life seemed richer, fuller, and more fun. Throughout high school and college his friends hung around the dock on days off, sometimes going out on someone's boat or driving off in a pickup. They were always full of plans . . . always drinking beer. The boys were always giving me compliments, too . . . some cheeky, which always brought a laugh to my lips. But they were always polite and grateful when I showed up with my special peanut-butter brownie recipe.

Miller was sixteen years younger than Taylor. He idolized his older, handsome, broad-shouldered big brother. He hung around Taylor and his friends like a mascot. Most boys would've been annoyed, but Taylor enjoyed Miller's presence. Taylor's friends were likewise gentle with Miller and his feelings. They had to be, or face Taylor's wrath. He took his role as big brother seriously. As their mother, it was deeply satisfying to see their bond.

When Taylor went off to the Citadel, he was still close enough to come home when his schedule allowed. Once he graduated and accepted his commission in the Marines, however, Taylor had truly left home. His commitment was as steadfast as his sense of duty. Over time I sensed him shifting his focus from his family and friends—even his girlfriend, Ashley—to his band of brothers. He'd let go of my hand.

Then his deployment to Afghanistan was announced. Everyone in the family reacted differently. Miller was excited. He was too young to be fully aware of the dangers. In his mind his older brother had soared to new heights. Alistair had accepted it with a southern man's pride in his son's fighting for his country. Me? I was proud, of course. But I'm his mother. I simply could not reconcile my son's going to fight on hostile soil. I'd rather he'd stayed home, safe, and worked in the family business as we'd hoped. But Taylor had always been clear he'd had his sights set elsewhere. Alistair had accepted this and argued that I should, too. But what mother was glad that her son went off to war?

I did what mothers of soldiers have done for centuries. I prayed. I had always prayed for my children, yet during the year of Taylor's deployment I prayed morning, noon, and night that my baby would come home safe. I clung to my faith, believing my prayers were heard. What else could I do when I felt so helpless? I was also vigilant in following news of the war, getting information from wherever I could.

Then my worst fears were realized. In the middle of a summer night my heart had stopped when we received word that Taylor's convoy had encountered an IED, killing all the men in the truck that hit it and seriously injuring others in the convoy. I'd read about the carnage caused by IEDs in Iraq and Afghanistan—how they were a game changer in the war. So when I'd learned Taylor had been thrown from his truck, suffered several fractured bones and burns, but had survived, I fell to my knees in gratitude and wept. He was alive. Injured, but bones would heal. My son was coming home.

After his discharge from the hospital, I'd hoped he'd come home for Thanksgiving. But instead he went to Oregon to visit a Marine buddy. That was hard, I admit. But good things come to those who wait, right? Now it's my turn. Taylor was coming home for Christmas. Today!

At the appointed hour, the family climbed into Alistair's pickup and headed for the airport. Driving separately was Ashley, Taylor's girlfriend. Everyone else stayed behind at the house for the big surprise. Once at the airport, I felt the final ten minutes standing outside the security gate lasted longer than the months I'd waited for Taylor's return. At my left, Alistair stood stoically, his big arms crossed over his slight paunch, his mouth set, and his gaze never leaving the gate. Miller was bored, dragging the hand-painted welcome sign as he walked aimlessly around the airport. He'd grumbled at least twice how he wished he had an iPad.

In contrast, Ashley was talking on her phone to a friend, her eyes lit up with anticipation. She was wearing a cherry-red coat that only someone young and trim could pull off. The color accentuated the paleness of her golden hair, curled loosely down her shoulders in the current

style. Her manicure was perfect, as was her makeup. I felt a bit self-conscious and glanced down at my pressed navy pants, polished-but-worn black boots, and my plain black wool coat. I wore a bright red scarf for holiday color, but it seemed dowdy compared to Ashley's. When I looked
up, I met Ashley's nervous gaze. Suddenly it didn't matter what I was wearing. I felt older and wiser seeing the vulnerability in her eyes, and smiled encouragingly. Of course Ashley would be dressed to the nines. That poor girl had been in love with Taylor since middle school.

I glanced at the arrival board to confirm Taylor's plane had landed. Anxious, I took a few steps forward, meriting a warning glance from the guard. Several people were walking down the exit ramp, a sure sign the plane had released passengers. Ashley put her phone away and came closer to the gate, eyes glittering. She reapplied her lip gloss and checked her reflection in her pocket mirror.

At long last I spied Taylor coming our way. He had to be one of the last off the plane. I sighed with relief when I didn't see the cane he'd been using. He was dressed in civilian clothes, required for an off-duty Marine. I would've recognized his gait anywhere—steady, sure, shoulders straight. My eyes roamed his face hungrily. His hair was cut short in the high and tight style of the military, and his green eyes were searching the crowd. I knew the moment he saw me; Taylor missed a beat, then walked faster toward us with a smile on his face.

I stood breathlessly, bound at the gate with open arms as he grew nearer. Squinting and leaning forward, I scanned his lean, tan face, seeking out scars and finding none. In a final stride he dropped his bag and wrapped his long arms around me. I hugged him close, shutting my eyes, feeling hot tears flow down my cheeks. My boy was home. Safe in my arms. God had answered my prayers. I stepped aside and, wiping my cheeks with my palms, watched as Alistair stepped forward in a handshake that morphed into a hug. Finally, Miller couldn't hold back any longer. He drew near, then stopped short, uncharacteristically shy. Taylor extended his arm to include Miller. I took a step back, overwhelmed with emotion to see my three men together again, wrapped in a single embrace.

A few feet away Ashley hovered, fingertips pressed to her lips. Taylor hadn't seen her yet. When he released his brother, he turned his head and his eyes widened with obvious surprise. He opened his mouth but Ashley rushed into his arms, looping hers around his neck, and began crying. Taylor put his arms around her and lowered his head to speak into her ear, but it wasn't a tender moment. Nor was it the bear-hug, lift-her-off-her-feet kind of hug she'd expected him to offer. Despite his smiles and polite words Taylor appeared somehow . . . reserved. As if he were going through the motions.

In that moment I thought of my hug. I'd shed tears and hugged tight, but Taylor had felt rigid in my arms. His chest was as hard as a rock, but more, I hadn't felt any reciprocal emotion. I narrowed my eyes and watched as he spoke to Ashley. He stood tall, arms crossed before his chest. Ashley was like a fluttering bird, touching his arm, laughing a bit too much. Was he overtired? In pain? He appeared strong and healthy.

But a mother knew. . . . Something was different about him. I couldn't put my finger on it. A withdrawal. A distance. A mother knew. . . . Taylor hadn't really come home.

Our contract is an old one. It was made when we were both poor and content to be so, until, in good season, we could improve our worldly fortune by our patient industry. You are changed. When it was made, you were another man.

—Belle, *A Christmas Carol*

Chapter 6
Taylor

It was the same drive from Charleston to McClellanville I'd driven countless times before. Over the Ravenel Bridge, following Highway 17 north up the coast. Christmas lights glowed in the dim light of dusk. All I could think about was getting back home so I could go to my room, shut the door, and pull myself together.

Ashley drove me in her Jetta. She'd recently purchased the car—her first new one, she told me, and she proudly pointed out all of its features. Mardi Gras beads hung from the rearview mirror, and Coldplay blared from the speakers, a welcome change from carols. During the nervous, break-the-ice minutes of our first time alone together in over a year, Ashley rattled on and on nonstop, updating me about friends we used to know, places where we used to hang out, and how Charleston had grown up from the quiet town we loved to a chic metropolitan city. I'm not partial to change and was sad to hear that. At length Ashley ventured to ask me about my experiences in the war, but I'd grown adept at cutting off this line of inquiry with short, noncommittal replies.

We passed through Mount Pleasant, then

Awendaw, to the sign that instructs you to turn right to McClellanville. As we drove along the darkened, winding road toward the coast, Ashley fell into a tense, exhausted silence.

I welcomed the silence. I was fighting a splitting migraine brought on by the stress of being confined in a small space on the plane and the emotions of the family reunion. Not to mention seeing Ashley Cooper again. For the past fifty-five minutes as I listened to her chatter on, all I could think was, *What are you doing here?*

"You don't seem very happy to see me," Ashley said accusingly, breaking the silence. She swung her head to look at me, her face more a pout than a scowl. The pout was her signature move.

I studied her face in the pearlescent light of streetlamps to gauge her meaning. Ashley was a true southern beauty, peachy skinned with finely arched brows and full lips. *Kissable lips,* the guys called them, and for years I'd made sure I was the only man to kiss them.

"It was nice of you to come meet my plane."

"Nice of me?" Her voice rose. Her fingers tapped the wheel in agitation. "Of course I would come to meet you. You're my boyfriend!"

She sounded hurt, but it wasn't my intention to cause her pain. "I didn't realize I was still your boyfriend."

"Why would you think that?"

I shook my head with a short laugh of disbelief.

"Maybe because of the Dear John letter you sent me in Afghanistan."

"I never sent you a Dear John letter!" She glared at me again and met my gaze. After a moment's impasse her expression changed to guilt. She waved her hand dismissively. "Oh. *That*. That wasn't a Dear John letter. I was simply writing to tell you that since you were gone for such a long time, I thought we should, you know"—she lifted her shoulders—"start dating other people."

"In my book that's breaking up."

Ashley looked at me again, brows furrowed, then abruptly pulled to the side of the road. We were only a block from the house, but she parked at a haphazard angle and, with an angry twist of the wrist, turned off the engine.

I rubbed the bridge of my nose with my fingers, then my temples, trying to ease the throbbing before the confrontation. Were we really going to do this now?

She took a deep breath, then turned in her seat to face me, all her previous joviality gone.

"Then you should have told me that," she cried. "See? That's what's so frustrating with you. You don't tell me what you're thinking. I'm not a mind reader. If you didn't want me dating anyone else, it would've been nice if you'd told me that."

"Look, you wanted to date other men. I got that."

"Yes . . . No . . ." She shook her head and put her face in her palms. "I don't know."

Tears came then and it pained me to see them. Literally. My head throbbed. "Don't cry."

She dropped her hands. The blue of her eyes shone like sparkling lakes, and for a moment I was transported back to the time when those eyes lost in tears had me under her spell. There was a time I would've done anything for her.

I wished I could still feel that passion.

"I was lonely!" she cried. "You were always away."

"I was fighting a war."

"I know," she said, mollified. "But I was here. Waiting. Always waiting." Her eyes flashed. "You didn't give me anything to wait for."

I closed my eyes and ground out, "What does *that* mean?"

"When you graduated from the Citadel, I thought, '*Now* he'll propose. We'll get married as we'd planned.' I waited . . . but you didn't. You went right off to the Marines, and then I only saw you on occasion. I'll be honest. I went out with a few guys then. Just dinner. Drinks."

My eyes flashed open.

"Nothing happened," she hurried to add. Then she lifted her chin. "It could have, but I stayed true. Then before you got deployed, I thought, 'Now he'll propose. He'll want me to have something to hold on to. A commitment. A promise.

Something! He won't leave me with nothing to hope for.' " She shook her head and said with anger, "But you didn't! Once again you left me behind." She sniffed and brusquely wiped the tears from her face. "So I wrote you that letter. I'll have you know, Taylor McClellan, that a lot of people consider me a catch. I've waited long enough. I'm past my prime! I have to take care of myself, too. So, yes, I've been dating other men."

The challenge in her eyes shifted to defeat. Her lips shook. "But here's the problem. You're still stuck in my heart. What am I supposed to do, Taylor? Tell me. Help me. What am I supposed to do?"

This time Ashley dissolved into tears and slumped against my chest. My heart ached for her but still I stiffened, wanting to pull back. Sympathy gave me the strength to put my arm around her and gently pat her shoulder as she clutched my shirt and sobbed. The feel of her rounded shoulders, the smell of her hair—memories flickered. Yet there were subtle differences. Her hair was shorter now, styled more maturely. Her life had changed, as mine had. Ashley had a new job, a new car, new interests. New friends. She didn't fit in my arms the same way anymore.

I had a hard time with people touching me because of my PTSD. Even hugging my parents at the airport was a concentrated effort, but I wanted to hug them. To feel them close. Perhaps it was because I didn't want to hug Ashley that I realized I didn't love her.

I looked out the windshield at the streetlight ahead. White fairy lights entwined the pole with pine to join a bright red bow at the lamp. Cars and trucks lined both sides of the street. Someone was having a party.

Ashley's words were true. I'd treated her badly and deserved her anger. "I never meant to hurt you. I've always loved you. And in some way, I always will." I pulled back her shoulders and gave her a moment to lift her face to meet my gaze. Hope was shining in her eyes and I could see that she expected me to propose now. The timing was right. I was home again. Honorably discharged. Ready to settle down. This was what she'd come for.

I knew what I had to do.

"But I'm not the same man you once loved. I'm not the man who left home. I'm damaged goods."

"No, don't say that," she rushed to say. "You just need time. I could help you."

I shook my head with finality. My voice was low and firm. "You can't. No one can. I have to do this alone."

"I've waited before. I'm good at that." She ventured a quick smile. "You'll get better, I know you will. You're one of the lucky ones. You survived. You're home now."

I felt a flare of anger at hearing myself called a lucky one. The question of why I survived and my buddies didn't haunted me.

"*Did* I survive?" I said with a bitter laugh. My voice turned cold. "The jury's out on that. Listen, Ashley, what I'm trying to tell you is—go ahead and leave me. No blame. I want you to."

I saw the shock on her pretty face. And the hurt. "You don't mean that," she whispered.

"I do. And . . . ," I said gently, "it's what you really want." I offered a half smile, reasoning with her, reassuring her. "That *was* a Dear John letter. And it's okay. I deserved it. You're here now to say good-bye. I only hope we can part as friends."

Ashley stared back at me and I could see that she was weighing my words, trying to believe them. I'd given her a graceful out. I let her break up with me. She could save face.

"Friends . . . ," she said softly, tasting the words in her mouth. She disentangled herself from my arms and smoothed out her coat with brusque movements, almost as though she were brushing away any remnants of my touch. She swallowed, then looked at me, her eyes flashing. "I don't know if I can be your friend, Taylor. Or want to. Not after . . ." Her lips trembled and she bit them to stop the break in her voice. But she rallied. I was proud of her. "If this is good-bye, I want a clean break. I don't want to see you again."

That hurt, and it surprised me. I manned up and let her go. "Understood."

Ashley's eyes widened slightly at the finality. Then she sniffed and withdrew to sit behind the wheel again. She put her hands on the wheel and, after exhaling a long breath, said, "We should go." She started the engine and put the car in gear.

"Ashley . . ."

She turned to look at me again. This time her eyes were cold. Vacant. It felt that it had been much longer than a year since I'd last seen her. More like I'd never known her.

"You'll understand if I don't join the party," she said tersely, looking out the window. Her face was the picture of hurt mixed with resolve.

I swung my head around, filled with dread. "The party?"

She met my gaze with a grimace. "Oh." Then, with only faint remorse, she added, "It was supposed to be a surprise."

I groaned and put my throbbing head in my palms. I was torn. I couldn't drive off with Ashley, that bridge was burned. On the other hand, I wasn't sure if I could endure the convivial chatting and cheers of a welcome-home party.

"How many?"

"Fifty of your nearest and dearest. The old gang, neighbors, friends of your parents. Everyone's excited to welcome you home." She averted her gaze out the window.

I stared down the street at the cars lining the road and thought of chatting and smiling with all those people. I'd rather face down an army of insurgents.

"I'll get out here," I told her, sparing us both the short drive in an awkward silence. Ashley deserved the chance for a quick exit.

"Suit yourself."

I stood in the cold, darkened street and watched Ashley pull away. As the red rear lights disappeared from view, I felt as though a huge chunk of my past drove off with her. Maybe the best part of my life. I felt numb inside. I looked over my shoulder to check out the area, then, tucking my hands into my pockets, I turned and made my way down the street.

I stopped at the curb of my parents' house, where shadows of men and women filled the windows. The sounds of laughter and carols flowed from inside, filling me with anxiety. My heart started pounding like a locomotive in my chest, and I fought the urge to keep on walking. I thought of my mother and all the work she must've done to arrange this party, and stayed.

I was trained to do my duty regardless of personal pain. I bent my head, clenched my hands in my pockets, and made my way along the crooked walkway toward the white cottage with the wide covered porch, up the wood stairs festooned with holiday swag, to the front door.

Squaring my shoulders, I raised my fist to knock. I entered my childhood home.

"He's here!"

When I stepped into the house, a cry of "Welcome home!" arose that could rival any Marine battalion's *Oo-rah!* I froze as I was barraged by a throng of well-wishers. Women in clouds of perfume hugged and kissed me; men heartily slapped my back and shook my hand, boisterously asking why I wasn't in uniform, wanting to see my chest candy. Standing close by, my father obliged them, proudly reciting my list of medals and commendations. I wanted him to stop embarrassing me. A hero? Hardly. I felt undeserving of those medals and racked with guilt that I didn't bring every man under my command home safely this Christmas.

I was led to a table groaning under the weight of lowcountry food. It being McClellanville, there was no shortage of freshly harvested shrimp. Mama had made her world-class pickled shrimp in red sauce, knowing it was my favorite and a Christmas staple in our house. There was the classic Frogmore Stew with shrimp, corn, and spicy andouille sausage, she-crab soup, Hoppin' John black beans and rice for good luck that was usually served at the New Year, the requisite barbecue, sausage balls and assorted deviled eggs, boiled peanuts and pimento-cheese sandwiches. Someone handed me a huge plate overflowing with food; another pressed a beer into my hand. I checked out my surroundings, looking to the left and the right, found an empty chair, set down the plate, and drank the beer thirstily.

I hadn't been in my home for over two years. In the old house people stood shoulder to shoulder, laughing, drinking. The house was decorated for the holidays; my mother's touch was in every nook and cranny. Yet I felt far away from the home of my youth, separated from everyone, even loved ones, by a thin, gauzy veil.

And I felt trapped. My face was suffused with heat, kindled not by the warm room but growing panic. I felt the rooms closing in on me and a sudden urge to flee.

"Hey, buddy, how 'bout a beer?"

Startled, I looked up to see my old high school buddies—Jack, Teddy, Wes, Woody. I broke into a wide grin and rose to clasp hands and receive hearty hugs.

"Let's get out of here," Woody said, and jerked his head in the direction of the back door.

We escaped the party and the incessant carols and moved to the backyard, stepping into the blast of cold air. I gulped it down, welcoming the bracing chill after the stifling crowd. I could feel the sweat chilling my brow and felt my breathing ease. In the distance the trees lurked ominously and I barely made out Jeremy Creek racing silently with the tide. Together we collected wood, gathered branches and lit a bonfire. We stood around it, watching the flames flicker in the night, shooting the breeze as we always had while chugging down beer after beer. My headache began to ease with the alcohol and the fresh air. And I felt more comfortable now in the shadows.

But in time, despite the light of the fire, I felt the inner darkness creep over me again, advancing with the pounding of my heart. I again felt isolated, the odd man out. I didn't belong in this party of revelers. Step by step I moved back several paces from the fire into the shadows. From a distance I drank beer and let my gaze scan the faces of men who were at one time my best friends, men I'd shared so much of my life with. They rocked on their heels, laughing and sharing memories of our antics in high school. We'd done everything together back then. It seemed more than a lifetime ago. Even though we went to different colleges, we'd hung out at home during the holidays and summers, bound by a brother-hood that had begun in diapers. But after college graduation only I had joined the service. Only I went to war, while they continued their lives in South Carolina. Not that one choice was better than the other. Just different. My gaze traveled from face to face and I wondered if their experiences on their individual paths made them, too, think from time to time that they were different. Hadn't we all changed from the carefree youths we once were?

I took a long sip of my beer, downing it to the dregs. Lowering my hand, I stared at the empty bottle and realized that no amount of beer would change that I was now different from these boys. I tasted bitterness in my throat and threw the empty bottle far into the darkness. It landed with the satisfying sound of glass shattering.

Who was I kidding? I was an old man compared to my friends. I'd seen things, done things, that they—that no one at home—could understand. The chasm between those who'd witnessed the atrocities of war, who had stared death in the face and survived, and those who had not was as dark and murky as the ocean.

I stepped closer to the fire, feeling its heat. Listening to the laughter of these men who were alive to enjoy this Christmas, I felt alone with my thoughts and my guilt for the men who wouldn't be returning home to their families this Christmas. As the sparks from the fire swirled up to mingle with the stars in the vast sky, I said a quick prayer to whichever God was listening for the souls of those brothers I'd left behind. And that I'd find the strength and courage to find my way through the black mist I was lost in back home.

Hard and sharp as flint, from which no steel had ever struck out generous fire; secret, and self-contained, and solitary as an oyster.

—*A Christmas Carol*

Chapter 7
Taylor

The party was winding down when I made my escape to my room. I closed the door, leaning against it with my head bent and panting like a pugilist who'd made it through twelve rounds. I didn't turn the lights on. Rather, when I could move, I found my way through the darkness of my childhood room to the bed and fell back against the mattress. It was as lumpy as ever and I was grateful for it. I lay with one leg hanging over the side of the bed and my arm over my eyes, trying to slow my breathing and stop the roller coaster of my emotions. It took all I had to hang on. I couldn't speak to one more person. Hear not one more thank you. Not one more good-bye.

A short while later an unwelcome knock came on my bedroom door. My muscles tightened, poised for flight. I forced myself to lie still and ignored it, hoping whoever it was would just go away.

No such luck. A young and inquiring voice called from behind the door. "Taylor?"

I didn't answer.

"You in there?" More insistent this time: "Taylor?"

"Go. Away," I growled back.

"Mama said you're to come downstairs and say good-bye to your guests." Miller sounded reproachful. When I didn't respond, he said, "So get in trouble. See if I care."

I couldn't blame Miller for being annoyed. I heard his footfalls retreat and descend the stairs in angry thumps. I lay on the bed, unmoving, exhausted, praying for sleep that I knew wouldn't come. I hadn't slept well for months. I only had a long series of fits and starts clustered around horrific memories and worse nightmares. Why did the doctors think coming home was a tonic? No one here understood what I was going through. At least in the VA hospital I was among guys who were going through the same terrors I was. We didn't need to talk about it. We read the communal histories in our haunted eyes.

A short while later I heard another soft rap on my door. "Taylor?"

I softly groaned, hoping my mother would just go away.

I heard the door creak open, and a shaft of light from the hall wedged into the room.

"Taylor, are you asleep?"

"No."

"Can you come down, just for a minute? Your guests are leaving."

"No."

"Honey, you don't want to be rude."

“I have a splitting headache,” I ground out, my frustration and pain audible.

There was a moment’s pause, then a soft, apologetic “Oh. Okay.” I heard the door close with a soft swish of movement.

I closed my eyes and concentrated on willing my bowed-up muscles to relax.

Hours later I still wasn’t sleeping. I was lying in my childhood bed, feeling as lost and alone as any preadolescent. And just as afraid. The walls were closing in on me. I rose up on my elbow and reached over to turn on the bedside lamp.

Rubbing the crick in my neck, I surveyed my old room in the soft light. I’d inherited the four-poster full bed from my grandfather Morrison McClellan, a famed shrimp boat captain who was lost at sea. I’d painted this room myself, the Citadel blue and navy colors, in my senior year of high school in a burst of excitement after getting my acceptance letter. Over the bed I’d hung the insignia of the Marine Corps in a place of honor when I accepted my commission. The painted pine dresser that had held my elementary-school clothes now held the new civilian clothes I’d purchased since my honorable discharge. They were neatly folded, the socks were rolled, my war medals were polished. This was the discipline of the Marines I’d been trained in.

One window overlooked the front of the house and the narrow road that, if you turned left, led to the docks and the *Miss Jenny*. If you turned right, it would take you to Pinckney Street. I rose from my bed and walked to the back window, crossed my arms, and looked out. The trees, shorn of leaves, appeared as cragged fingers in the moonlit night of winter. The mighty Jeremy Creek was merely a blue mist in the distance. But in my mind's eye it raced, glistening, under brilliant-blue skies. How many hours had I spent looking out at the creek winding its way far out through the waving grass on its way to the Intracoastal and the ocean beyond? How many dreams had I had, standing at this window, of traveling far beyond the borders of McClellanville, of South Carolina, even the South?

If I had known then that I'd travel to the other side of the world, to a place far from my beloved sea, to where water was scarce and sand dominated the horizon, would I still have gone?

The answer came readily. Yes. I was proud to have served my country. Yet standing here now, I knew that war was never the glory-filled battlefields of a boy's dreams. War was beyond the imagination of a boy. Back here in my old room—a boy's room—I mourned the loss of my innocence.

How did I end up back here? I wondered in weary dismay. All that I'd worked so hard for, all my dreams and ambitions, had been blown away that day in the Humvee along with my comrades. This broken body was still alive, but my spirit . . . my soul . . . had died that day.

In a sudden flash, the memories of that day flared up in my mind with the force of a bomb. I fell back onto the bed, my palms over my face as though to block out the view. But nothing could erase the images from my mind. They were branded on my brain, searing memories of smoke and screams, of burning rubbish and dismembered bodies. Dropping my hands, I pushed up to sit on the side of the bed, feet on the floor, elbows on my knees, feeling the heat scorching my body and sweating profusely. I rocked back and forth, a soft keening in my throat.

God help me, I was out of Afghanistan, here on US soil. Why couldn't I shake the anxiety and stress of life in the war zone? I lived in perpetual fight-or-flight mode. It was a cruel irony to be in my childhood room where I'd once felt safe, when my instincts told me to remain vigilant, wary of everyone. The welcome-home party had taken every ounce of my hard-won discipline and waning energy so as to keep a stiff smile and make even the briefest utterances and replies. Clutching my blanket, I felt my anxiety levels rising off the charts. I knew I had to lie low, to cling to some semblance of control. I had to remain in my cave. Fight-or-flight was an instinct developed by humans in response to danger since the days of the cavemen. It was either that or get eaten alive.

The last guest had finally left and the house was quiet. I lay on my bed as the last vestiges of my panic attack eased and I could breathe normally again. My mouth felt like cotton. I needed water.

The scent of pine and cinnamon potpourri floated in the darkened hall as I followed the glow of under-cabinet lights in the kitchen. Stepping into the room, I stopped short, surprised to see my mother standing at the sink with a teakettle in her hand. She spun around at the sound with a gasp.

"Taylor! I didn't hear you."

"Sorry. I didn't mean to startle you."

She seemed flustered, even nervous, clasping her robe close at the neck. It was the first time we'd spoken to each other without a crowd of people around us in over a year.

"I couldn't sleep. I'm making a cup of tea." She raised the kettle in her hand. "Would you like one? Chamomile will help you sleep."

I shifted my gaze to the back of the kitchen, where I knew my father used to store his stash of booze. "I'm looking for something a little stronger."

"Oh. Well, there's beer in the fridge."

"Doesn't Daddy usually have a bottle of bourbon around?"

Her smile slipped. "Uh, yes," she stammered. "But I don't know how much is left after the party. It's over . . ."

Her voice trailed off as I was already walking to the far cabinet by the rear windows. Many nights in high school I'd sneaked a swallow from the bottles I found in there. If my father had ever discovered the levels of his amber liquid lowered, he never questioned me about it. Opening the cabinet, I almost smiled with relief. There were two bottles of Jack Daniel's, one almost finished, the second unopened. I reached for the full bottle.

I could feel her eyes tracking me. It made me nervous. "This'll help." I indicated the bottle in my hand. I headed toward the door and my escape.

"Don't you want a glass?" she asked.

"I'm good."

"How's your headache?" Her voice was full of concern. "That will only make it worse. Dehydrate you. Do you want some aspirin?"

"Got some."

"Taylor?"

I stopped to look over my shoulder. Even in the low light I could see worry etched across her tired face. She'd grown thinner. Her face had a few new lines.

She said comfortingly, "Are you all right?"

No, I wanted to tell her. *I am not all right.* I was anything but all right. My hand squeezed the neck of the bottle and I tried to allay her fears with an attempt at a smile. "I'm just tired. I, uh"—I ran my hands along the short, stubby hairs on the crown of my head—"I wasn't expecting a party."

"Oh." She was crestfallen at the implied criticism. "I wanted to surprise you."

My head thrummed and I felt my thirst for bourbon intensify. "You did."

She smiled weakly, unsure of how to take that. "Well, go on to bed." She gave a quick wave of her hand. "I hope you feel better in the morning."

I nodded curtly. Just that small gesture sent ricochets through my brain.

As I walked from the room, I heard her voice call out behind me, "I'm so happy you're home!"

The happiness he gives is quite as great as if it cost a fortune.

—A Christmas Carol

Chapter 8
Jenny

The following morning I made a breakfast fit for royalty, which to me Taylor was. Lots of thick bacon, home-baked corn muffins, and fluffy eggs. I poured myself a cup of coffee, breathed deep its heady scent, and looked for the hundredth time toward the stairs.

"When's he coming out of his room?" Miller asked, reaching for a muffin.

Alistair glanced at me, equally curious.

"When he's ready," I said, taking a sip of coffee. "He isn't feeling well."

"He must be dead if he can't smell that bacon," Miller said.

"Don't say such a thing!" I said, appalled. "Why, that was heartless. His being alive is an answer to our prayers."

"Sorry," Miller mumbled, muffin crumbs flying from his mouth. I couldn't be too angry with Miller when I also thought the scent of bacon would have drawn Taylor out.

"Is he just going to sleep all day?" Miller wanted to know.

"He's just returned from war. With injuries,"

Alistair said sternly. “He can sleep as much as he damn well wants.”

Miller’s eyes narrowed at being reprimanded.

“Eat up,” I said to Miller. “You’ll be late for school.”

“Yes, ma’am.” Miller glanced at the clock, then pushed back his chair and rose, sticking another piece of bacon in his mouth. “Gotta go.”

“Your lunch!” I shouted after him, a paper bag in my hand.

Miller grabbed the bag, enduring my kiss the way only a ten-year-old can.

“Come straight home after school.”

“I wanna go to Dill’s.”

I shook my head. “Not today, honey. It’s your brother’s first day home.”

“Mama . . .”

Alistair lowered his newspaper and said with finality, “You heard your mother.”

Miller’s face darkened, but he nodded in compliance before stomping out the back door.

I grabbed the dirty dishes and carried them to the sink. “He’s still holding out hope for that puppy. I can’t bear to think of him going back there and playing with him again. It’ll be too hard on him.” My hands stilled at the sink and I turned to face Alistair. He was reading the paper again. “I’ve got some money put aside. It’s not enough, but if I don’t buy you anything for Christmas, and you don’t buy me anything . . .”

Alistair snapped the newspaper shut and set it on the table. He said in measured tones, "You know buying that dog's the cheapest part of owning it."

I turned back toward the window. "I suppose. But we've always made do before."

"No, Jenny."

I heard the warning in his voice, but I couldn't let it go. I turned toward him. "He's such a good boy. . . ."

Alistair shut his eyes for a moment, pained. "Don't you think I want to buy him that dog?" He opened his eyes. "You know all the boats are hurting now. The captains are trying, but they can't give me enough work. As it is, I'll probably have to go to Florida in January."

"Oh, no . . ."

Alistair's face was creased with despair and he said loudly, "What else can I do?" He paused, then lowered his voice. "I didn't want to tell you this till after Christmas. I kept hoping something would turn up." He met my gaze. "We could lose the house."

The sponge dropped from my hand. "Not the house. But how?"

"The usual way," he said darkly. "When you don't make the payments, they foreclose."

I slumped against the sink, filled with dread and a new fear. I let my gaze sweep over the kitchen, my colorful pottery collection on the shelves, my sweetgrass baskets collected over many years. I gazed out the windows facing the river. I couldn't lose my house . . .

"I'm trying," he said, a flush creeping up his neck. "I'm looking for carpentry work, handy-man jobs, anything I can find. But it's tough during the holidays. People put house projects on hold. I feel like I'm banging my head against the wall every day, going around town with my hand out."

I could see in his face how demoralizing this was for him, a man once held in the highest of esteem.

His voice rose. "Hell, yes, I'd like to get my boy a dog! But we can't add anything more, hear? Not one thing. We're hanging on by our nails." He looked down at his hands and added with a roughness in his voice, "Miller might as well learn now as later that life is tough. Money don't come easy."

I didn't respond. I hoped my boy would never have to learn that harsh lesson. When Alistair was in this mood, I'd learned that it was best to let him settle himself down rather than corner him. He was quick to flare and his temper was fearsome, but he was also quick to cool.

He reached out to me. I sighed, recognizing the movement as an apology, and swiftly crossed the room to step into his embrace.

"We'll get by," he said reassuringly. "We always do."

"I can try to get more cleaning jobs. Demand picks up during the holidays. I'll put the word out."

"I never meant for you to clean houses."

I closed my eyes and breathed in the salty scent of his skin. Back when shrimp was king, I ran a small shop by the dock to sell product to the public and a few local restaurants. There was shrimp, of course, but I also sold a few specialty items such as my cheese straws, key lime pies, stone-ground grits, and lemons. During the holidays my pickled shrimp in red sauce did a good business. We weren't rich, but we brought in enough so I could be close to home when Taylor and Miller were young. And the shop gave me my own niche in the close-knit shrimping community that I could be proud of. Though shrimpers were independent by nature, they banded together when the chips were down. Their wives were like that, too. Always at the door with a hot dish and a helping hand when someone was sick, a baby was born, or a family member died.

When the imported shrimp began being dumped on local markets at a ridiculously low price, the local shrimpers began to feel the pressure of a shrinking market. I hung on as long as I could, but eventually I had no choice but to close my shop. I didn't know what else I could do for work. Substitute teaching was spotty at best. When a friend asked me to help out in her housecleaning business I thought it was good money, and I was accustomed to hard work, so I agreed to give it a try. With each passing day, the temporary position was becoming more permanent.

"It's good, honest work," I told him.

He gave me a tight squeeze. "I don't want you to buy me anything for Christmas. If you have some money set aside, buy something for yourself. God knows I can't get you anything nice."

I saw the regret wash over his face and slipped my arms around his neck and kissed his cheek. I whispered, "I don't want anything from you that I don't already have right here in my arms."

He squeezed me harder, holding me near. "I don't know how you put up with me."

I felt my heart lurch and kissed his cheek again. The skin was freshly shaved and leathery. He was a proud man. A good man. I slowly rose, letting my hands slide from his shoulders. "I don't either," I quipped.

I laughed and returned a sloe-eyed glance when he reached out to playfully swat my retreating bottom.

"The school is not quite deserted," said the Ghost. "A solitary child, neglected by his friends, is left there still." Scrooge said he knew it. And he sobbed.

—*A Christmas Carol*

Chapter 9
Taylor

The afternoon was waning, but my hunger wasn't. For the past several days I'd avoided the family, grabbing food when the coast was clear and bringing it up to my room. I found fewer ghosts lurked in my dreams if I slept in the daytime. I splashed cold water on my face, and lowering the towel, I caught my reflection in the mirror. I hardly recognized myself. My hair was growing back, looking as if a beaver pelt covered my calp. My jaw, too, was covered with the dark stubble of two days' growth.

I slipped into my robe, put a pack of cigarettes in the pocket, and made my way downstairs. The scent of pine lingered in the living room where swags hung at the mantel. Signs of Christmas were everywhere—my mother's collection of Santas on tables, bowls of pinecones and holly were everywhere, a kissing ball hung in the foyer. I could see and smell the cheer of the season, yet none of it reached my heart. As I walked toward the kitchen, I heard a muffled groan coming from the dining room. Curious, I followed the sound to find my little brother hunched over the table, chin in one palm, a pencil in his other. A book and lined paper were strewn over the table.

"I hate this book," he groaned, and tossed the pencil across the room.

"Need some help, pal?"

Miller swung his head and looked at me with surprise that quickly shifted to uncertainty. I knew I looked like a homeless reprobate. I probably smelled like one, too. I had always been an early riser, early dresser, never letting the sun catch me unready. Seeing repugnance and not the swift shift to joy spark in his eyes that had always been his hallmark when he spotted me, back when I was his hero, hurt me more than anything else had in a long while.

"You're up," he said with more sarcasm than I'd expected.

"Yep." I ignored his tease. "You're home," I added as a rejoinder.

"Got out early today."

I nodded in understanding. Coming closer, I looked over his shoulder at the papers on the table. "What are you doing?"

He rolled his eyes and turned back to the papers in front of him. "A book report," he said.

"I always hated doing book reports, too. What's it on?"

"A Christmas Carol."

"I read that. Good ol' Charles Dickens. It's a good story."

He shrugged. “It’s all right, I guess. I’m only halfway through it.”

I chuckled. “It’s not a long book,” I teased.

“It is to me.”

“Come on. What’s not to like? It’s a classic. It’s got ghosts, great characters, Christmas, and it’s short.”

“It’s not that. It’s the questions.”

“Mind if I look?”

With a loud sigh of resignation, he waved his paper at me in a desultory manner.

I took it and sat beside him.

“You stink.” Miller wrinkled up his nose.

“Yeah, I know.” I looked at the paper. “Questions?” I asked, humor laced with criticism. “You only have to answer one.”

“I don’t get it!” he exclaimed with frustration.

“Take it easy, Bro. Let’s see.” I read aloud, “ ‘Describe what Marley meant in the passage below.’ ” I looked up to make sure I had Miller’s full attention. I continued to read:

> *“You are fettered,” said Scrooge, trembling. “Tell me why?”*
>
> *“I wear the chain I forged in life,” replied the Ghost. “I made it link by link, and yard by yard; I girded it on of my own free will, and of my own free will I wore it. Is its pattern strange to you?”*
>
> *Scrooge trembled more and more.*

"Or would you know," pursued the Ghost, "the weight and length of the strong coil you bear yourself? It was full as heavy and as long as this, seven Christmas Eves ago. You have laboured on it, since. It is a ponderous chain!"

I paused and, like Scrooge, felt the implication of Marley's heartfelt warning in my own heart. His words, though couched in the jargon of the nineteenth century, rang clear and true. Yet it was no wonder that a boy of ten couldn't yet understand the depth of meaning in the words. What boy understood the full impact of regret?

Miller waited for my answer.

"What do you think Dickens meant by the chain Marley was dragging?"

"His sins?" Miller asked.

I rubbed my jaw, the stubble tickling my palm. "Yes, his sins," I began. "But I think he also means his choices. We all have free will, right?"

Miller nodded.

"So, whenever we make a decision, a choice, we make it freely. Right or wrong, it's ours to live with. Marley was reminding Scrooge that we have to live with the consequences of our choices. And after death, atone for our bad choices."

"Like in hell?"

"Yes." As I said the word, I thought of the hell I was living in as a result of my own decisions. I wore the chain forged of the souls of men I'd lost in the war. It was heavy, indeed. A ponderous chain. I would drag that burdensome chain, crying out in the wind for eternity, like old Marley.

"Taylor?"

Miller's voice drew me back from the hell I was slipping back into. I wiped my face with my palm and looked at my brother, forcing myself to deal with the present. Miller's eyes, blue like my father's, were guarded, sensing the mercurial shift in my emotions. I thought back to the last time I'd seen him. So trusting and eager to please. When did he learn sarcasm? I wondered. What caused him to be so wary? He was still so young. As yet so innocent. I wished in that moment that I could protect his innocence forever.

I suddenly needed to get up and have a smoke. "Where's Mama?" I asked abruptly. "She used to help me with my book reports."

"She's still working."

"At the shop?"

Miller looked back at me with puzzlement. "The shop?" he asked incredulously. "She closed the shop years ago."

I stared back, stunned. "Closed it? Why didn't she tell me?"

"She probably didn't want you to know. She never wants anything to upset *you*."

I didn't miss the dig. "So, what's she doing now?"

"She cleans houses."

I remembered seeing the new lines on her face and noticing how she'd lost weight. Yet she never complained.

"When does she get home?" I looked at the ladies clock on the sideboard. It had always been important to my mother to be home when I returned from school. Miller was only ten and he'd returned to an empty house. Or, nearly empty. I was suddenly ashamed of sleeping all day.

"She's usually home by now. I guess she got busy," Miller said without blame. "She's been working extra hard lately, taking on more houses."

"Why?"

"She had to. With the boat and all."

My attention sharpened. "What about the boat?"

Miller looked at me as if I were the ten-year-old. "It's docked. Sheesh, Taylor, don't you know any-thing?"

I stared back at him, stunned by the news. "Apparently not. Tell me."

Miller leaned back in his chair and shrugged. "Dad couldn't afford to keep the boat on the water anymore. So he docked it."

"Dad's not shrimping?" I asked, shocked.

Miller shook his head. "Nope." His tone held no small measure of the superiority he felt knowing the family business while I, obviously, was in the dark.

I rubbed my hand across my scalp and exhaled. How little I'd kept up on family news; the extent of my estrangement hit home like the blast of a boxer's blow. I was speechless and felt sure my face showed it because Miller spoke up.

"We're poor now," he said matter-of-factly.

I snorted with disbelief. "What?"

"We're poor," he repeated without a smile.

His simple acceptance of that fact shamed me. I paused, collecting my thoughts. "Why didn't anyone tell me what was going on here?"

"Why didn't you ask?"

I laughed at my own hubris. I was worse than Scrooge, oblivious of anyone's needs but my own, as stingy, barren, cold, and empty as they were.

"This is quite a Christmas," I mumbled, looking around at the cheery decorations and thinking of all the pain and scarcity they masked.

"Yeah. And you're supposed to be my Christmas present," Miller said, clearly not thrilled with the gift.

"What?" I asked, clueless.

Miller sat up in his chair, his eyes shining with emotion. "See, there's this dog, this puppy really, that I really want. I mean, *really* bad. I watched it grow up since it was born, and he's six weeks old now. I asked Mama and Dad if I could have him for Christmas. I even offered to give them all my money. Seventy-five dollars! But they said no. *Daddy* said no," Miller amended. "And you know Mama. She won't go against what Daddy says."

"Why did Daddy say no?"

"He says we can't afford a dog."

That seemed miserly. "How much is it?"

"Three hundred dollars, but Mrs. Davidson said I could have him for two hundred dollars because she could see how much Sandy . . . that's the puppy . . . loves me. She says Mama has to say yes, though, or she can't let me have him. And Daddy says we can't afford a dog. That's what I mean when I say we're poor. And I hate it." Miller pushed the papers away from him in an angry shove and buried his face in his arms on the table.

"Mrs. Davidson is Dill's mom? I remember Dill. You two were inseparable," I said, remembering. "Mutt and Jeff." I looked over at Miller, his head still in his arms.

"So his dog had the puppies?"

Miller lifted his head to nod. His eyes were shining with tears. "His mama's dog, Daisy. Dill is getting to keep one of the puppies for himself," Miller added reproachfully.

"What kind of dog are we talking about?"

Miller sniffed and wiped his eyes, eager to talk to someone about his dog. "A Labrador. Daisy is brown and she had six brown puppies and one yellow. That's the one I like. He's the biggest, too. I call him Sandy Claws because of his color and it being Christmas and all."

I saw Miller's love for the dog shining in his eyes and thought, *How can Daddy not buy Miller this dog?* "Maybe Mama doesn't think you're old enough to take care of a dog. She's already working hard. I'm sure she doesn't want to add picking up puppy poop to her list of chores."

Miller snorted with feigned disgust. "She wouldn't have to lift a finger. She knows that." His face hardened. "It's Daddy. He says we can't afford to take care of it. He says that about everything now."

I watched his face harden and felt regret. Miller used to idolize Daddy. My brother loved working on the boat with him and always claimed he wanted to be a shrimp boat captain, just like our daddy. I was sorry to see his disillusionment.

I rose and reached for the cigarettes in my pocket. "You never know." I patted his shoulder. "Santa might surprise you."

Miller's face fell. "If you mean Daddy, don't count on it."

"Finish this here homework assignment." I tapped the paper with the tip of my finger. "I'll take a look at it when I come back in." I lifted my cigarettes. "I'm going out for a smoke."

“Yeah, whatever.” Miller reached out to slide the homework paper to his side of the table.

Before I left the room, I cast a final glance at Miller. He sat in the same slump-shouldered position over his paper as before, but at least now he was writing.

Out on the porch I lit up and felt the comforting burn in my lungs. I stood in the chilly afternoon air looking out at Jeremy Creek. But all I could see was the hope bubbling in Miller’s eyes when he told me about Sandy. I exhaled a plume of white smoke in the frigid air. I wanted to be his hero again.

I wear the chain I forged in life. I made it link by link, and yard by yard.

—Marley, *A Christmas Carol*

Chapter 10
Jenny

The next two days flew by as I worked extra houses and extra hours. The sky was already dark when I got home. I pushed open the back door into the kitchen, relishing the blast of warm air. My buckets filled with dirty rags rattled noisily as I set them on the floor with a weary sigh. The last house had been a large five-bedroom overlooking the Intracoastal, and the missus was having a holiday party that weekend. She wanted everything "spruced up." I explained that I'd have to charge extra for "deep clean" items such as the chandelier and baseboards, but that didn't seem to bother her in the least. I couldn't imagine having so much money you could just get what you wanted when you wanted it. Truth be told, I didn't want to spend the extra time working today. I'd pushed hard without lunch or a break for both scheduled houses, hoping to get home by three to check on Taylor. He'd holed himself up in his room and I was getting worried.

I pulled the check from the last house out from my coat pocket and looked at the amount. I couldn't help but smile with satisfaction. My back might ache but at least now I had the extra money for a nice Christmas dinner. I hummed "Christmas Time's A-Coming" and set to gathering the dirty rags, then headed to the laundry room.

When I returned to the kitchen, I stopped short, surprised to see Taylor standing in front of the open fridge. His green military-issue robe hung open over his boxers and T-shirt. He had a hole in one of his socks. Seeing him standing in that familiar pose staring into an open fridge—one I'd seen so often when he was a teen—I had to laugh.

Taylor spun around at the noise, bumping the fridge door with his elbow and rattling the contents. He held a half gallon of milk in his left hand.

"I guess it's my turn to startle you!" I'd never known him to be so jumpy. He looked disheveled, unshaven, as if he hadn't showered since he'd arrived. "I guess we'll have to get used to seeing each other roaming the house."

Taylor smiled nervously as he set the milk back in the fridge and closed the door. "Yeah," he replied self-consciously, tying the belt of his robe at his waist.

"Are you hungry?" I walked briskly into the room and went directly to the sink to wash my hands. "I can make you a sandwich. Pulled pork sound good? I've got mountains left over from the party."

"Yeah, that sounds good. Thanks."

We switched places at the fridge. So close I

couldn't miss the smell of bourbon that emanated from him like a dark cloud. I began pulling out ingredients from the fridge, happy to be making him a meal again. "Did you eat today?"

"Uh, I grabbed some chicken from the fridge earlier. It was good."

"That's your aunt Betty's special marinade. I've asked her a million times for the recipe. I swear, she'll go to the grave with it." I kept up the chatter while I opened the bread, sensing Taylor's uneasiness. It troubled me to see him so ill at ease in his own home. He used to light up the room when he walked in, filling it with his personality. This sullen man with hair shorn like a sheep, who spoke in monosyllables, I didn't know.

While I heated the pork in the microwave, I kept an eye on Taylor as he walked to the rear windows. He was much thinner than I'd first surmised. He'd changed dramatically, I realized, feeling a sinking in my stomach. I could see his sharp bones where muscle used to be, and his chiseled cheekbones protruded now, making his face appear gaunt. But his eyes were what disturbed me the most. His pale green orbs were rimmed with dark circles, making them appear bruised. In the explosion he'd hurt his back, broken bones in his ribs, his left arm and leg, but I didn't fully see until now that my son was indeed a survivor.

Well, he is home now, I thought to myself with a

mother's resolve. *I just need to fatten my boy up.* I heaped another scoop of potato salad on his plate, and then cut two buns in half. I'd be serving dinner in less than two hours, but I wasn't sure he'd show up. He rarely did. "You feed the dog when the dog barks," I muttered.

From the corner of my eye I caught sight of Taylor pulling out a pack of cigarettes from his robe pocket. I didn't know he'd started smoking and was sorry to see it. He put the cigarette in his mouth.

"Smoke outdoors, please," I told him, adding firmness in my voice.

Taylor took the cigarette from his mouth. "Sorry."

"Nasty habit." I scrunched my nose to show my displeasure as I placed a few of the holiday cookies on his plate. "It'll kill you."

"I should be so lucky," he mumbled.

The words stung, and I swung my head to stare at him, unnerved. The Taylor I knew would've never said such a thing. The microwave beeped, calling me to fetch the pork, so I let the comment drop. What was there to say, anyway? Instead I held my tongue and kept myself busy preparing the hot sandwiches. The Carolina pulled pork and onions that I'd slow-cooked smelled heavenly, reminding me that I hadn't eaten since breakfast. I set the two sandwiches on the plate beside the potato salad, a large pickle, and the cookies.

I called Taylor to the table: "Come sit!" I set the plate down, then hurried to put salt and pepper by his side, double-checked that he had a napkin, then stood watching as he lowered into the chair and picked up the sandwich.

"Looks good." He stared at the plate. "It's a lot of food."

"You're far too thin. And pale," I added.

"I was just thinking the same about you."

"What?" I laughed, self-conscious, and smoothed my disheveled hair. "I just got off work. I must look a mess. Besides, I'm just getting old, that's all. But you!" My eyes caressed his gaunt face, saw his long, thin legs exposed where his robe fell open. "I've got to fatten you up. Hold on, I'll get you a glass of milk." A minute later I set the glass on the table and stood beside him, hands clasped together. I couldn't help myself. It had been so long since I'd served my son a meal at the kitchen table.

Taylor stopped chewing and looked at me. "What?" he asked, mouth full.

I frowned at his boorishness, and flustered at being caught staring, I quickly looked away. "Nothing." I smiled weakly. "I just can't believe you're sitting here. At my table again."

His brows gathered as he swallowed hard, set the sandwich on the plate, and wiped his mouth with a paper napkin. "Gotta tell you, it's kinda creepy you just staring at me."

I flushed, uncomfortable with the awkward tension between us. It felt so foreign. "Indulge your mother," I said jovially, and reached out to set my hand on his shoulder. As much to reassure myself as him that all was well. I felt his muscles flinch at my touch. I pulled back my hand as if I'd been burned, then hurriedly retreated across the kitchen to fetch a glass. My hands shook as I stood at the sink and filled the glass with cold water, then brought it to my lips. I was so upset I could hardly swallow. That he would flinch at my touch cut me to the core. I sneaked a furtive glance at Taylor from over the rim of the glass, trying not to be caught staring. He'd returned to his sandwich. *Who is this man?* I asked myself again.

I set the glass on the counter and tried again, saying nonchalantly, "I didn't see Ashley at the party."

Taylor shook his head, his eyes on his plate. "She went home."

Talking to him was like pulling teeth. I leaned against the counter and looked again at him from behind.

"But why? She helped me plan it. Corralled all your old friends. She was so excited. Poor thing, was she sick?"

"No. We talked and she wanted to go home."

"Oh, no, did you have a fight?"

Taylor swallowed hard. "No, we didn't have a fight," he answered, piqued.

"She's such a nice girl. I've always liked her. I always hoped that, well, you know, that you and she would tie the knot one day. You've been together forever."

He put the sandwich on his plate and turning leveled his gaze at me. "We broke up, okay?"

I fell silent. I'm sure my face showed my disappointment because he turned back to the table. During the party preparations I'd secretly dreamed of Ashley and Taylor's getting back together now that he was home, maybe even getting married and having children. Weren't those all the things a mother hoped for her children?

Mercifully, the telephone rang. I hurried to answer it.

"Hello?"

"Hey, Mrs. McClellan. It's Jack."

"Jack!" I turned to face Taylor. Jack had been the closest of Taylor's group of friends, a kind of brother. Surely Jack would be able to break through the ice barrier that Taylor had created around himself. "It was so good to see you the other night. Long time. Too long! Thanks for coming."

"Sure. Wouldn't miss it for the world. Great to see Taylor again. Hey, is the old boy around?"

I met Taylor's gaze, eyebrows raised in question.

Taylor scowled and shook his head.

I couldn't keep my opinion from my face. "Oh, uh," I stammered, uncomprehending why Taylor wouldn't want to talk to his best friend, "I'm sorry, Jack. He's sleeping now. He's not feeling well. . . . What? Oh, it's probably just the flu. You know how it is with air flights." I rolled my eyes. I was a terrible liar. I didn't think Jack believed me. "Sure, I'll tell him you called. Love to your mother. Bye."

I lowered the phone and looked pointedly at my son. "Jack wants you to call him back."

Taylor looked at his plate.

"Oh, and he mentioned something about a party."

Taylor answered fast, like a knee-jerk reaction. "I'm not going to any party."

"Oh, honey, you need to get out of this house. See your friends."

"I don't want to go out."

"But why not?" I replied, in almost a whine. Then with encouragement: "It would do you good."

Taylor didn't respond, but he shifted in his chair.

"If you're not ready for going out with your friends, maybe we could do some Christmas shopping together. Maybe even go to Charleston. Wouldn't that be fun?"

He lowered his head and put his fingertips to his forehead. "I don't want to go *anywhere,*" he said with a flare of anger.

"Oh." I took a breath. "You don't have to get snippy."

"Mama . . ." There was a tone of apology. Taylor paused, then dropped his hand. His eyes squinted against the light. "I have a blinding migraine."

My anger fled, replaced with concern. "I have some Tylenol."

"I eat fistfuls of stuff like that and it doesn't do anything."

"It might be the flu. There's so much of that going around now. And you've been traveling. Have you seen a doctor?"

Taylor burst out a short laugh. "Yeah, I've seen a doctor. I saw one right before I came here. He wouldn't give me any more pain pills. He's afraid I'll get addicted." Taylor snorted as if that were preposterous. "So now I'm left to suffer and begin all over again with a new set of doctors in Charleston." His hand slammed the table. "What's the point? They don't fix anything anyway."

"Here, let me check your forehead." I walked closer to put my hand on his forehead. He waved it away brusquely. "I'm just checking to see if you have a fever."

"I don't have the flu. Or a fever. Look." He held my gaze. "My bandages are off, but the injuries are still there. In my head." He tapped the side of his head for effect. "In my brain.

That's why I have migraines." Taylor pushed the chair back and climbed to his feet.

"Wait," I cried, shooting my arms out in an arresting motion to stop him from leaving. He pushed past me. "Taylor," I cried, a knot forming in my throat. "Don't push me away. Don't push your friends away!"

Taylor spun on his heel, his face coloring. "They're not my friends!" he shouted back, hands in fists at his thighs. "My friends are dead. And it was my fault. Mine! I was the officer in charge. I was responsible for them. And they died. You tell me why I'm alive and all my friends are dead!"

I stared into his eyes, so tortured with guilt and unspeakable sorrow. My heart was breaking to see him in such pain. "Oh, Son, it's not your fault."

He swore under his breath and headed out of the room.

"Let me help you!" I cried.

"You can't!" he shouted back.

I watched him retreat down the hall, heard his heavy footfalls on the stairs, and flinched at the slamming of his bedroom door. My breath released in a shuddering sigh as my arms dropped to my sides.

"Mama?"

I swung around to see Miller standing at the back door, his blue wool scarf wrapped around his chin up to his open mouth. He'd returned home from school. His eyes were wide with fear and confusion. "What's the matter with Taylor?"

I shook my head and ventured a weary smile. "I don't know, honey." I walked to Miller's side and put my arm around his shoulder. The parka was cold but I was grateful Miller didn't flinch. "I don't think he knows, either."

No warmth could warm, no wintry weather chill him. No wind that blew was bitterer than he, no falling snow was more intent upon its purpose, no pelting rain less open to entreaty.

—*A Christmas Carol*

Chapter 11
Taylor

I was back in Afghanistan. I stepped out from my barracks into a blast of heat. It felt like stepping into an oven and I was the turkey, all trussed in my body armor and helmet. Sweat began pouring down my back, my forehead, stinging my eyes.

"Let's load up," I ordered. Me and thirteen other men climbed into assigned Humvees in the long convoy. Doors slammed shut. Someone in mine yelled out to crank up the AC. It was just another day in the sandbox. Another routine tour of the perimeter. We took off with a jolt. Jon was strapped in the gunner's turret. The merciless sun baked the landscape, turning it a hundred shades of yellow. Dave was sitting next to me, telling me how he was going home for Christmas and who was going to be there, and all I could think was that he had a helluva big family. Then he told me what they'd eat for dinner, elaborating about his mother's chocolate bombe cake. He described it with loving detail—the rich chocolate center, the whipped cream on top—I wanted a taste of that cake so bad and told him so.

Then he took off his helmet, just to wipe his

brow. It was against regulations, but what the hell. It was just for a minute. One minute I was looking at his face, and the next I heard a deafening explosion and was flying. Then everything went white. I couldn't hear anything but the pounding of my heart in my ears. I blinked but couldn't see anything.

"Dave!" I shouted, my throat burning. A fine dust filled the air and my lungs. I could hardly breathe and coughed my guts out. I tried to struggle to my knees but my back was twisted and I screamed with pain.

Panic swelled with helplessness. I was vulnerable. I couldn't see, couldn't hear, I was hurt. But my sense of smell was working overtime, picking up the acrid and pungent scents of diesel fuel, burning rubber, and something so bad it left a taste in my mouth. I rubbed my eyes and strained to see through the fog.

My sight gradually returned and I realized I was in a billowing cloud of smoke. As the smoke dissipated, I saw I was lying in my own blood, my leg bent at an odd angle. My back was twisted. But I could move my head. I saw bodies—parts of bodies—and burning metal chunks and wheels of what was once my convoy. Wreckage was everywhere. When I could hear again, the screams were deafening.

"Dave! Where are you?" I cried in a panic.

I looked wildly for my gun, groping around

my useless body. My heart pounded faster and my blood pressure rose and my muscles tightened. Suddenly I felt something in my hands. I grabbed it tight.

"Help me!"

"Taylor! Stop! Wake up!"

I heard crying and whimpering. I blinked hard, coming further out from the gray smoke. Through the haze I recognized my bedroom. Then I saw my mother's eyes.

"Mama," I said in a choked voice.

"Taylor, let go of me," she said tightly.

Awakening further, I saw that I was kneeling on the mattress and gripping her arms. My fingers sprang open as I immediately released her. She slumped back a few steps, rubbing her arms.

"Mama, I'm sorry," I managed, breathing heavily. I still felt the heat of the desert on my back, and my mouth was so dry I could hardly talk.

She was breathless with fear, still rubbing her arms. She looked at me with a combination of concern and caution. "You were having a nightmare," she said, trying to keep her voice calm. "I heard you cry out."

"I have them every night," I said.

I sat back on my haunches and mopped my face with my hands. When I realized where I was in my mind, in my crazed state, what I could have done . . . Just the thought that I could have really hurt my mother scared me like nothing before.

I swung my head up to look at her. "Are you all right?"

"Yes," she answered quickly. She reached over to the light and flicked it on. The golden halo of light was instantly comforting. "I'm fine." Then she stepped closer, albeit carefully, the way one would approach an injured animal. "But you scared me. Your eyes were wild. Like you didn't know me."

I sighed and shook my head. "I was still in my nightmare," I said in a low voice. "It's so real. I was back in the war." I could feel my heart rate speed up just remembering. "I was in hell," I said, ending it. I was shaking and needed to pull myself together. Looking up, I saw her stricken face watching me. I was scaring her. "You should go back to bed."

Her face crumpled in worry. "Will you be okay? Should I wake your father?"

"No. I just need to be alone." I looked at her and felt the weight of what I'd done. "Thanks for waking me up. I didn't know it was you. I'm sorry I grabbed you." My gaze raked her arms, studied her face, her stance. "Are you sure you're all right? Please tell me, did I hurt you?"

She rubbed her arm but shook her head. "You scared me more than anything."

"Mama, I'm sorry." My voice broke and I bent my head in shame.

"I know," she answered quickly, but she didn't come closer. "Will you be all right? I can sit up with you."

"I'm awake now. But, Mama"—I looked up and held her gaze—"I want you to promise me that if I'm sleeping and having a nightmare, you won't come near me. You won't let Miller near me. I don't know what I'm doing. *Promise me.*"

Her eyes were round with fear. "I won't. I promise."

I exhaled my fears and nodded. "Good."

Her gaze scanned the room. Clothes and trash were strewn about, and dirty plates from my scrounging through the kitchen. The room smelled of stale food and the telltale scent of cigarettes.

"Maybe later I can get in here and clean this place up. That'll help you feel better."

"I'll do it."

"I'm happy to do it."

"No!" I barked in a knee-jerk reaction, my voice so loud I startled her. I quickly collected myself and said in a softer voice, "I'll do it."

"Well," she said, at a loss for words, wringing her hands. "Okay then. I'll check on you later."

"I don't need you to check up on me."

"Don't you?" Her eyes flared as she pinned me with her sharp gaze. I'd pushed her as far as she'd go. Now she was my mother again, not taking any more insolence from her child.

"You're holed up in this room, not showering, not eating, having horrible nightmares. Smoking cigarettes when you know I don't allow smoking in the house." She reached out to indicate the near-empty bottle of bourbon on the bedside stand. "And all that drinking isn't good for you. It'll rot your liver."

I brought my shaking hands to the mattress and clutched it tight. "Right."

"Don't be smart with me. I'm still your mother." She paused as emotion welled up in her. "I don't like to see you so unhappy. You just need to pull yourself together, that's all. Clean yourself up. Go out some. Get a job. Snap out of it! You're such a great man. Your whole future is waiting for you."

"Stop it!" I barked out. Then, closing my eyes, I said softly, "Please."

Her lips opened, as though she were about to say something else, but thinking better of it, she turned to leave without another sound.

"Mama," I called after her.

She stopped and turned, her face appearing wounded.

I thought of how she cleaned houses for others to make ends meet, how she kept a tidy home, cooked for her family, woke in the middle of night when her son cried out. No matter how tired, she was always there, giving more of herself and never complaining.

"I'll shower tomorrow. And shave."

The lines on her face eased as she brightened. "Good. And then I'll come in here and clean your room."

I watched my mother leave, then grabbed the bottle of bourbon and drank it dry. Shower and shave, I thought bitterly. If only that would make me feel like my old self. The man I once was. I knew *that man* was the son Mama was still waiting for. Not this mean, angry, crazy man I'd become. I couldn't be touched. I couldn't go out. I couldn't get rid of the memories. Hell, I couldn't sleep. Get a job? How could I get a job, much less hold one down? I tossed the bottle into the trash bin.

Rubbing my palms together I felt desperation stir in my gut. I had to do something for money. I'd saved enough while in the Corps to keep me going for a little while. I'd lived modestly. But it was running out. After it was gone, I didn't know what I was going to do. I'd applied for disability four months ago and was still waiting. Who knew if I'd ever get a cent?

And I was a fraud. I didn't come home because of Christmas. I came home because I had nowhere else to go. I didn't know how tight money was for Mama and Dad. I wanted to help them, the way a good son should. Instead I was a burden.

Worthless. I couldn't stay with my parents forever. But what could I do? Where could I go? I only knew I couldn't go on living like this forever. Not in this hell. Not making the lives of my family hell.

My heart cried out with the anguish of Marley's regret. I thought again of the damned ghost's ponderous chain. The chain forged of his misused, miserable, miserly life. I fell back against the mattress, feeling the unbearable weight of the links of my own.

Darkness is cheap and Scrooge liked it.
—*A Christmas Carol*

Chapter 12
Miller

This was turning out to be the worst Christmas ever.

Everyone was on pins and needles and all because of my so-called Christmas present—Taylor. It had been over a week and still he stayed in his room most of the time, sulking, smoking, playing loud music, and using the Internet. No way my mother would've ever let me get away with that. I heard Mama arguing with Dad at night. Dad said Taylor just needed to shape up. Mama said he needed to see a doctor. That he was getting worse, not better. Me, I'm just getting mad at him for making everyone worry.

I caught Mama standing outside his closed bedroom door, her hand pressed against the wood, her ear close, listening, looking like she might cry. I knew she wanted to go in there to open the curtains and clean up the room, but every time she tried, Taylor barked at her that he just wanted to be left alone. I went up and knocked on his door a couple of times. I wasn't sure what to say, but his being my brother, I felt I should visit. But he never let me in.

The worst was when Daddy went in Taylor's

room last night. He'd just come back from a carpentry job. He walked into the kitchen to find Mama crying. Daddy puts up with a lot, but he can't bear to see Mama cry any more than I can. Then he saw the angry yellow bruises on her arms and got real angry. I mean, his face was as red as a beet.

"That's *enough,*" he'd ground out in that voice that always sent me running for cover. Daddy turned on his heel and headed to Taylor's room, mumbling words I could only catch on the fly, like *no kid of mine* and *not gonna put up with it.*

"Alistair, stop!" Mama called after him, but he wasn't listening. "He was having a nightmare!"

She hurried after Daddy down the hall. No one was aware of me close behind. My heart was pounding as hard as their footfalls on the wood floors.

By the time I got there Daddy had already pushed open the door and stormed into Taylor's room. Mama stood at the open door peering in. She held out her arm to keep me out. I peered in around her to see Daddy standing at the foot of Taylor's bed. Taylor sprang to his feet, alert, eyes glaring and arms out, poised to jump. Then he pulled himself back to stand erect, legs wide. He was still in his boxers and T-shirt. His beard was thicker now and the room stank like the cabin we used for hunting trips.

"Who do you think you are?" Daddy shouted at

Taylor. He was busting loose with all the tension he'd felt for days. "You dare hurt your mother?" He reached out and roughly pushed Taylor's chest.

Taylor stumbled back a few steps, then instantly reared up and put his fists up, eyes glaring. Next to me, I heard Mama suck in her breath.

Daddy didn't back down. He took a step closer and jabbed his finger right in Taylor's face. "Nobody hurts your mama. Nobody makes your mama cry, hear?"

I didn't say anything but I wanted to shout at Daddy that he'd made Mama cry plenty of times. But I couldn't speak. I held my breath as the two men glared at each other. They were evenly matched. He was the same height as Taylor and nearly as broad. Taylor might've been through war, but Daddy had had more than his share of fistfights.

Then Taylor dropped his hands and clasped them behind his back. He stared straight ahead, legs wide in a military stance, seeing no one.

"He didn't hurt me!" Mama shouted from the hall. "If you'd listened, I told you he didn't know what he was doing. He grabbed me in his sleep. He wasn't awake."

Daddy rubbed his jaw, his breath coming hard with anger, but I could tell he'd heard her and was reining himself in. He couldn't back down and had to save face. He looked around the room with disgust.

"Look at this place. It stinks in here! And you're a Marine? An officer? I wouldn't tolerate this kind of slovenliness on my boat, and I'm sure as hell not going to tolerate it in my home. What the hell's wrong with you, boy? You're making your mother cry, did you know that?"

Taylor flinched but he didn't respond.

"As long as you're living in my house, I want you up and showered and dressed like any decent person, got it? Then your mama's going to clean this pigsty. You'll help her. And you'll stop smoking in the house. After the holidays I expect you to start looking for a job, too. Not just for the money but the direction. You need direction, boy."

Taylor didn't move, but his eyes shifted and bore into our father's. "I've taken my last order. I'll pack up and leave by the end of the day."

I heard Mama gasp. "No!" she cried, stepping into the room. "It's Christmas!" She turned to Daddy. "Stop this fighting, hear? I won't have it!" To Taylor she pleaded, "Taylor, honey, you can't leave now. Please, you just got here."

Taylor frowned but said nothing.

Mama looked at Daddy again, her eyes begging him to say something.

Daddy adjusted his pants, stepped closer, and said, the anger gone from his voice, "We just want you to get out of this slump, Son. What you're doin' here just ain't healthy."

"You think I don't know it's not healthy?" Taylor responded with heat. "*I'm* not healthy." He took a breath. "I have PTSD."

I didn't know what it meant. I looked at Mama.

She had a puzzled look on her face that matched mine. "I've heard of it," she said. "It's a brain injury, right?"

Taylor squinted, then said simply, "Yes. It's a complicated disorder. It's different things to different people."

Daddy's eyes narrowed slightly and he said bluntly, "It's a mental illness."

"A mental illness?" Mama said, shaken by the term.

"I'm not nuts, if that's what you're thinking," Taylor said, unruffled. "But I've got issues. Clearly. Nightmares being one of them. They may improve in time, but they won't ever go away. Not completely."

"Uncle Tommy, Grandma's brother, came back from Nam with something like that," Daddy said. "He became paranoid and suffered headaches. He'd isolate himself in his woodshed. Days on end. We tried to help him. To get him to see a doctor but . . ." Daddy cleared his throat. "We lost him. . . ."

Mama gasped and her hand reached for Daddy's arm. "Don't say things like that. That's not going to happen to our son."

"Just sayin'. Better to know the devil you're

dealing with. Thing is, nobody called it PTSD."

"You don't know what you're talking about," Mama snapped at him. "Taylor's depressed, I can see that. But suicide? It's cruel to throw that ugly word out."

"Truth is," Taylor intervened in a dull voice, "some guys with PTSD do commit suicide."

Daddy waved his hand in arrogant dismissal. "Those doctors are handing that PTSD diagnosis out to anyone with a complaint because it's easy. Just a wastebasket diagnosis. I know what you've got. It's called shell shock."

"That's enough!" Mama said.

Taylor said nothing but his lips tightened.

"You're saying all this"—Daddy swung out his arm, indicating the disheveled room—"is on account'a your PTSD?" His doubt rang in his voice.

Taylor didn't answer but rubbed his forehead with his palm.

"PTSD is for sissies," Daddy said with bluster. "None of those namby-pamby excuses for you. You're better than that. You knew when you went to war you were going to dance with the devil. But you leave the devil there. You don't carry him home with you."

Taylor dropped his hand and glared at our father. "It's not like I have a choice," he ground out.

Daddy pointed at my brother. "You do! You're a

McClellan. We get knocked around three times before breakfast out on the boat, then stand up for the next bout. We're made of sterner stuff. And you're my son. You can do it. I know you can."

I could see Taylor shrink into himself. When Daddy pulls that McClellan card on me, it leaves me feeling like a loser, too.

"You know what we say on the boat—what doesn't kill you makes you stronger. Right? Remember?" Daddy was gaining steam, thinking he was winning the argument. He pulled his pants higher and shifted his weight. "Well, tell me it doesn't fit this situation we got right here, too." He jerked his head in a nod, then put his hands on his hips and released a long sigh, letting loose the tension he'd held in his chest. "Now do us all a solid, Son," he said, a marked change in his voice. The anger was gone now, replaced by concern and a bit of conciliation. "Go on and take a shower, shave, and make yourself presentable. It'd do you good to take a walk to the docks. Get some fresh air. Check out the trawler. Tell you what. Let's walk out together and take stock. You and me. Same as we always done. Deal?"

Daddy held out his hand.

Taylor stared at the outstretched hand for a minute. Then he surprised us. He didn't take the hand—instead he walked into Daddy's arms and hugged him. Daddy stood still for a second like he didn't know what to do. Then he wrapped his arms around Taylor in a tight bear hug, the kind that squeezes the breath right out of me. That's when Taylor began to cry. I've never seen my big brother cry, not even when he fell from a tree and broke his leg.

My mama pushed me back and closed the door, giving the men their privacy. She had tears in her eyes, too. And to be honest, I shed a few myself.

When Taylor came out of his room again, he'd done as Daddy asked. He was shaved, showered, and dressed. He looked handsome and Mama told him so, several times. She and I stood on the porch and watched as they took off for the dock, matching long strides down the narrow road. Oaks bordered both sides of the road beneath a gray sky with low-lying clouds. Leafless shrubs and yellowed grass clustered in their scrubby, wiry winter garb. It was a crisp December day. Two weeks until Christmas. We stood side by side and watched until they disappeared from view at the bend of the road.

Mama lifted her chin and sniffed the air. "Smells like rain," she announced, then looked at me to see if I agreed.

"Yep."

"All right, then." She tapped the railing. "I'll open up those windows and give that room a good airing out." Her eyes gleamed with anticipation.

Mama approached Taylor's room with the relish of a starving man before a feast. She donned her apron and rubber gloves, tied back her hair, and turned up the music. My mother is a force of nature when it comes to housecleaning. She put me to work carrying out baskets of dirty laundry, dirty dishes to the sink, and bags of garbage to the curb. She opened the curtains and windows wide and brought in buckets of hot soapy water. The wind whistled as it carried away the stench of depression from the room. I heard my mama hum as she scrubbed the floor, then sprayed the windows and washed them inside and out till they gleamed. By the time she was done, my brother's bedroom smelled like the great pine woods—and was about as cold. Finally she closed the windows again.

She removed the rubber gloves and held them dripping at her sides while she surveyed her handiwork. I knew that all that backbreaking work she'd done for Taylor was her gift to him. I reckoned Taylor might not see it that way now. But someday he would and be thankful. I was right proud of all she'd done. I turned to look at her face and saw hope shining in her eyes that the spotlessness of the room would somehow help to clean out whatever was mucking up Taylor's mind. She sighed, went out, and returned a moment later with a glass vase filled with clove-studded oranges, pinecones, and sprigs of fresh pine. "The finishing touch," she said, and smiled at me. Her face was so pretty, wreathed in all that hope and joy and love.

I had to smile back. Because that's what happens when the spirit of Christmas hits you. It's contagious.

The next day the rain that my mother had predicted fell in torrents. And Taylor's door was closed again.

I came home early from school because we were on exam schedule before the Christmas break. Even though it was only two o'clock in the afternoon, the sky was dark gray and a rare winter thunder rolled ominously in the clouds. I ran from the bus into the house, but I still got drenched. I took off my shoes and coat and dumped them in the front hall, then hurried to the kitchen, where the smell of fresh-baked cookies warmed the air.

"Cookies!" I exclaimed as I followed my nose to the kitchen table, where rows of them cooled on waxed paper. My mother's almond crescent cookies. My favorites.

"Those are for the cookie swap," she warned me.

"I don't want those other ladies' cookies," I whined. "I only want yours. You make the best."

She smiled smugly and shook her head. "You ought to go into politics." She tossed me a dish towel. "Dry your hair."

I smirked as I watched her make me a plate. She served it to me with a glass of milk.

"Take this to your brother, will you?"

My brother? She'd said it so casually, but I heard the tension in her voice. She was asking me to do what she was either afraid or unable to do herself. No amount of coaxing . . . or cookies . . . would lure him out.

"What about *my* cookies?" I felt ignored. I was tired of Taylor getting all the attention.

"Come back and I'll have your plate ready."

My mama ran a hard deal. "Is his door open?"

"No," she said lightly, looking into the oven at the cookies baking. "But it's a good excuse to get him out again." She rose and turned to look at me with a smile. "Don't you think?" she asked brightly.

I pretended that I bought it. "If your cookies don't do the trick, nothing will. But what a Grinch," I added under my breath as I slid off my chair. Grabbing the plate, I headed upstairs. He was just my brother, I told myself. A grumpy, lazy, kind-of-crazy brother, but my brother nonetheless. So why did I feel so nervous?

At his closed door, I thought of the chapter in *A Christmas Carol* where Scrooge saw his door knocker morph into the face of his old, and dead, business partner, Marley. Kind of gave me the shivers. To be honest, I was angry at my brother because I hoped that after Daddy and he went out to the boat together things would change. They'd get back to normal around here. But Taylor was back behind his closed door and we were all acting weird again. He might have been hurt by a bomb, but he made this house like a minefield for the rest of us.

I shifted the cookies and knocked. There was no answer. I tried again, harder this time. Still no answer. Now I was mad. I was getting bored with his act. I looked at the plate of my mother's famous almond cookies and, angry, stuffed one in my mouth.

"I got some cookies for you," I called out, taunting him with my mouth full. "And they're real good. If you don't open the door, I'm gonna eat them all."

"Go away."

What a jerk, I thought. If Daddy could barge in, so could I. I pushed open the door and walked in. It smelled bad again, cigarettes and stale food and body odor. He had his bedside lamp turned on so I saw him sitting on the side of his bed, with his back to me. His arm jerked when I walked in as he hid something under the blanket. I immediately felt weird, like I was barging in on something private.

"Uh, sorry," I blurted out. "I just wanted to bring you your cookies."

Taylor raised one hand to wipe his brow. He was sweating and I couldn't figure out why. He had the window cracked open and it was chilly in his room.

Taylor cleared his throat. "I told you I didn't want any cookies." His voice sounded tight and shaken.

Was he crying? I wondered. Again? I stood, frozen and embarrassed for him. I couldn't bear to see my older brother cry. He was the strongest, bravest man I knew. I didn't know what else to say so I simply walked to his nightstand and set the plate down beside the bottle of liquor. It was another bottle; barely any of the amber liquid was left. I was surprised to see a copy of *A Christmas Carol* there as well. I looked around nervously, trying to catch a glimpse of what Taylor was hiding under his blanket.

"I set the plate right here, okay? You can eat them when you want."

"Just go."

I felt a panic rise up inside me, the uh-oh feeling my mama used to tell me about. Something wasn't right. I didn't know what, so I kept talking.

"You're reading *A Christmas Carol*, too?"

Taylor didn't respond. He sat at an angle so I couldn't see what was in his hands.

"I'm almost done," I chatted on, looking over

his shoulder. "I'm at the part where the Ghost of Christmas Future is showing him his grave. It's kinda scary."

No response.

"Are you coming to the Christmas play? It's *A Christmas Carol*."

Taylor shook his head wearily. "No."

"I don't blame you. It's not going to be that good. But Mama's all excited. She's baking the cookies for the intermission."

Taylor deigned to look at me. His eyes were red-rimmed and sunken. "Aren't you supposed to be in school?"

I shook my head. "Exams."

He sighed and his shoulders slumped.

"Whatcha got there?" I lamely pointed to what he was holding.

"Nothing."

I took a step closer, my eyes narrowing in scrutiny. "Let me see." When Taylor moved to block my view with his shoulder, I said, "I'm just going to keep pestering till you let me see."

"Get out of here." He swung his arm indicating the door.

In that flash of movement the blanket lifted just enough that I caught sight of black metal in his left hand. "Hey, is that a gun?"

"What if it is?" Taylor snapped back.

"Can I see it?"

"No. Go on, get outta here."

"What is it? A pistol?" I stepped closer. "What are you doing with it?"

"I'm cleaning it."

I took a quick scan of the bed and floor and didn't see any cleaning equipment. Taylor had already left for the Marines before Daddy taught me to hunt. But I knew all about cleaning guns and I knew he was lying. He wasn't cleaning any gun. Now I was really scared.

"Can I hold it?"

"Don't be an idiot. No. It's loaded."

"It is?" I swallowed thickly. "You'd better unload it! Daddy says you shouldn't hold a loaded gun in the house."

Taylor laughed shortly at that, only I couldn't see what he thought was funny. Nonetheless he brought the pistol to his lap. I watched as he used his thumb to push the release, and a black magazine dropped into his hand. Then with his palm he swiftly pulled the slide back on the top of the gun and a single bullet went flying through the air to land on the floor. I immediately clambered after it.

"Leave it be," Taylor commanded. "Don't touch it."

I froze, then straightened and nervously crossed my arms across my chest. "I've never seen a magazine up close before. That's cool."

"Cool?" Taylor asked, flicking me an assessing glance. "It's not cool. It's a killing machine."

"So why do you have it here? You're not at war anymore."

He laughed shortly. "Aren't I?" Taylor picked up the magazine and stared at it a minute. "You're a good kid." Taylor was still looking at the gun. "A good brother. But you should go." He looked up, and though we didn't speak, I felt a surge of love in his gaze. And a farewell.

I took a few steps back, suddenly terrified for my brother. "I forgot your milk for those cookies," I told him. "I'll be right back."

"Don't come back."

"I'm coming right back!" I shouted as I ran from the room, purposefully leaving the door open.

I took off for the kitchen, my heart beating like a wild thing in my chest. I prayed Mama would still be in there, and mercifully she was standing at the table moving cookies from the baking sheet with a big spatula.

"Did you . . ." She stopped when she saw my face.

I ran into her arms, tears filling my eyes. I was so scared I could barely talk.

"Miller, what is it?" She dropped the spatula and put her arms around me.

"Mama. Taylor . . ."

Her voice went cold. "What about Taylor?"

I straightened and looked in her eyes. "He's got a gun."

Her face paled, and with a gasp, she grabbed

my shoulders. "You stay right here," she ordered. "Call your father. But if you hear a gunshot, call 911."

Without another word, she ran out of the kitchen. I hurried to the phone across the kitchen. My hand was shaking so much I could hardly dial. Hearing my father's voice at the end of the line, I wanted to weep with relief.

"Daddy!" I choked out. My voice was raspy, like I'd been running.

"What's the matter?" He was instantly alert.

"Mama said to call you. Taylor's got a gun."

"I'm on my way."

The phone went dead. I hung it up and waited by the kitchen entry, staring up the long flight of stairs for several minutes. Those were the longest minutes of my life. There was no way I could stay in the kitchen. I was compelled closer, climbing up the stairs one by one, cringing at each creak, holding my breath. When I reached the top of the stairs, I stopped and clutched the wood post, clinging to it, real tight, like I was adrift in a stormy sea and if I let go, I'd drown. It was an angry day, spitting and whirling in a fury of wind and rain. There would be flooding, I thought. I hoped it wouldn't slow Daddy down, that he would make it home fast. I listened to the wind wail and craned my neck to hear the occasional voice from behind the closed door. Sometimes Mama's. Sometimes Taylor's. Just when I thought I couldn't wait a minute longer, I heard the front door burst open. My father rushed in, rain dripping from his hair down his face, his clothes soaked.

He stood at the bottom of the stairs, staring up at me. "Where's your mother?" His eyes blazed with worry.

I pointed to Taylor's room.

Daddy bolted up the stairs. I leaned far to the side, out of his way, then hovered again perched at the top of the stairs. Daddy pushed open the door and I caught sight of my mother sitting on Taylor's bed, her arms around him as he wept. She looked up when Daddy stepped in and slowly lifted her arm. She had the gun in her hand. It's ugly, cold metal caught the light.

I rose to my feet, my hand resting on the stair railing. Daddy looked back and, seeing me there, quietly closed the door behind him.

Would you so soon put out, with worldly hands, the light I give?

—The Ghost of Christmas Past,
A Christmas Carol

Chapter 13
Jenny

I watched Alistair drive away with Taylor. They were going to the VA hospital in Charleston to get Taylor the help he needed. When the car disappeared, I let my fingers drop from the curtain and slipped down onto the sofa and buried my face in my palms. I wanted to cry, but I was too tired for that much emotion. I was exhausted emotionally and physically.

I slumped on the sofa and rested my head back as a wave of anguish washed over me. How could my son be so miserable, so despairing, that he'd want to take his own life? Even though when I took the gun from his hands and he'd sworn he wasn't going to pull the trigger . . . who really knew?

I was a failure as a mother. No matter how much love I showered on my son, it wasn't enough to stop his feelings of helplessness. Or the nightmares. I'd felt sure that being home again, surrounded by all our love and support, would fix him.

I lifted my head and took a sweeping gaze of my home. The living room was draped with pine and holly. I felt the sting of disappointment. At this season when we should have been coming together as a family, we were falling apart.

"Mama?"

I jerked around to see Miller standing in the hall. Then I felt a sickening wave of self-reproach. With all the worry over Taylor I'd forgotten all about him, my second-born.

He pushed back a shock of his brown hair from his forehead. "Mama. I don't feel good."

I rose and hurried to his side to wrap him in my arms. *Poor Miller,* I thought. His stomach was probably tied up in knots after all he'd just been through. Taylor was being taken care of. Now I needed to worry about my baby.

"You're probably just upset about Taylor. I'm sorry you had to go through that."

After a pause Miller asked haltingly, "Was he going to kill himself?"

I looked at Miller with a mother's eye. He looked pale, with dark circles under his eyes. Such a horrid question for a child to ask. I swallowed my guilt that he'd seen and heard more than a ten-year-old should have. How could I explain such complex matters in a way Miller could understand but not be frightened? He was too bright for me to gloss over the facts. He deserved my honesty, I thought, even if simplified.

"I don't know. He was thinking about it. But, honestly? I don't think he would have gone through with it. You interrupted him at just the right moment. You were his guardian angel." I said a quick prayer of thanks that Miller had arrived when he did.

"Why's he like that?" Miller cried angrily, cringing in my arms. "He's acting weird. It's like the same guy didn't come home." Miller choked back a cry. "I don't like him anymore."

I squeezed Miller tight, brokenhearted to hear him say that about the older brother he'd once adored. Yet at the same time understanding. What reassuring words could I offer him when I, too, no longer recognized this stranger? I took a breath and spoke in as calm a voice as I could muster.

"I know you're having bad feelings about Taylor that are hard to admit, but that doesn't mean you don't love him, right?"

Miller shook his head.

"We have to remember it's not his fault. You're right. He's not himself. Your brother has something called PTSD. That's short for post-traumatic stress disorder. Try to understand that he's seen horrible things in Afghanistan and he can't get them out of his mind. The bad thoughts keep coming back, even when he sleeps. He has nightmares."

I could feel Miller nod against my chest. "I hear him."

I closed my eyes. How could he not? Miller

slept down the hall from Taylor. "He's going to the doctor's office now. They'll help him. He needs some medicine that will help him feel better and sleep." I released Miller, then lowered to meet his gaze.

His blue eyes looked back at me, filled with worry.

"Don't be angry with your brother. Try to understand and be patient with him. He's in pain. Wouldn't you want help if you were in trouble?"

Miller leaned into me, resting his head against my breast. I put my hand on his head, holding him close. "We have to be strong for him now. Like he was strong for his country. He's our hero, don't forget."

"Okay, Mama."

Miller stepped back and released a long, shuddering sigh. One that spoke of how long this bubble of anxiety had been in his chest.

"Can I watch TV?"

I normally wouldn't let him watch TV on a school night, but we all needed to find some relief today. I wanted a glass of wine but wouldn't have one until I'd heard from Alistair.

"Sure. . . . Did you eat lunch?" When he shook his head, I said, "I thought not. You must be starved. Do you want me to make you a sandwich?"

Miller scrunched up his face. "I'm not that

hungry." He seemed depressed, exhausted. His arms hung listlessly.

I stooped, kissed his cheek, and then ruffled his hair. "Go on, now. Just relax, okay? It's been a tough day for all of us."

Feeling helpless, I watched him climb the stairs to his room. My baby was afraid and lost, and the best I could offer him was a sandwich? I shook my head, fed up with my fantasy of how a good mother should behave. The belief that I could fix whatever ailed my sons if I just loved them enough, fed them good food, was a myth.

The PTSD was taking a heavy toll on my family. Taylor was getting help. I decided that it was beyond time for me to get professional help as well. I needed to learn about PTSD and how I could help Taylor. Letting him slip into isolation wasn't healthy. I could no longer expect his anger, mistrust, and depression to simply go away. Allowing Miller to be confused and frightened was unacceptable. And for me to continue giving easy answers and blithely telling everyone that everything was going to be okay was naïve. This was my home. I felt determined to do what I could to increase my loved ones' sense of comfort and—I had to be realistic—safety.

I went to Alistair's office and sat at his desk in front of the computer. Turning it on, I began to search for articles on PTSD. I hadn't realized how many there were. I settled in and began to read.

Two hours later the phone rang. Thinking it might be Alistair, I lurched for the phone.

"Hello!"

There was a pause, no doubt because I'd almost shouted, then a woman's voice. "Hello, this is Clarissa Black from Pets for Vets. Is . . ."

I silently groaned, thinking how I couldn't deal with a soliciting call now. "We're not interested," I interrupted, and began to hang up the phone.

"Wait! Please. I'm calling for Taylor McClellan. Is he there, please?"

When I heard Taylor's name, I hesitated with my hand midair, then brought the phone back to my ear. "I'm sorry; I thought you were some solicitor. Who did you say you were?"

"I'm Clarissa from Pets for Vets. We provide service dogs for returning veterans. Taylor submitted an application months ago. I'm following up."

"Service dog?" I was completely surprised. I'd just been reading about service dogs on the Internet. There were so many heartfelt stories from vets who claimed that having their service dog had changed their lives. She had my full attention. "Taylor asked about a dog?"

"Yes, he did." She paused. "Are you a family member?"

"Yes, I'm his mother."

"Okay," she replied, accepting that. "To be honest, I'm surprised he didn't talk to you about this. We encourage applicants to get the whole family involved. The dog becomes a member of the family."

Suddenly it all became clear. This was someone who could help Taylor. I gripped the phone, eager to talk to this woman. First, however, I glanced over my shoulder to make sure Miller was out of earshot.

"I've read about this. The dogs can wake them up when they're having nightmares."

"That's one of the many things they do. There are different kinds of service dogs trained for different needs. The blind, for example. I work specifically with dogs trained to help servicemen who've returned home with PTSD."

"And my Taylor applied for a service dog, you said?"

"Yes. A few months ago."

"So long ago?"

"Actually, his case moved along quickly. It's a long, complicated process." She paused. "And I have some good news for him. Is Taylor there?"

"No, I'm sorry he's out. He's at the doctor's. I'm not sure what time he'll be back." I debated whether to tell her what had happened, but I didn't know how much Taylor had confided in her. So I opted for less is more.

"Could you ask him to call me? As soon as possible. He has my number."

"Of course." Then I blurted, "Clarissa?" I hesitated. "Taylor's been having a very hard time. Very hard." I could feel my emotions welling up and my voice beginning to shake. I took a breath. "Will this dog help him out of his depression?"

"That's our hope. We work very hard to make that happen." Her voice grew filled with compassion. "These dogs are not pets, Mrs. McClellan. They're companion animals that can be the life-saving therapy that many returning servicemen and women need."

I felt the tears welling. "You have his dog, don't you?"

There was a pause. "Please, have him call me back."

I hung up the phone and almost fell to my knees in a prayer of thanks. Something in her voice told me that, yes, she had Taylor's dog. The timing was too close to be coincidental. This was an answer to my prayers! My Christmas miracle.

"Ghost of the Future!" he exclaimed. "I fear you more than any spectre I have seen. But as I know your purpose is to do me good, and as I hope to live to be another man from what I was, I am prepared to bear you company, and do it with a thankful heart."

—Scrooge, *A Christmas Carol*

Chapter 14
Taylor

Bundled gloomily in my wool coat, sitting slump-shouldered in the passenger seat of my father's car, I stared out at the passing world in silence. We passed the buildings, shops, and houses that I knew as a child, feeling as if I were a kid in trouble again. Worse, a total failure. Not just in my eyes, but in my father's eyes. My father had always been the man I'd looked up to, the captain I'd tried to impress. I'd measured my success by the gleam of approval in his eyes. I'd basked in his gaze. There was a time I was his pride and joy.

I closed my eyes and saw instead the image of my father sitting in the waiting room of the hospital when I was released. He had filled the small chair and sat hunched over, his elbows on his knees, his big, ruddy hands holding a pitiful paper cup of cold coffee. He wasn't reading. He was staring out with a blank expression on his face. When I'd approached him, he'd risen slowly, and when he faced me, I saw despair, confusion, even fear, clouding his pale blue eyes.

"I'm sorry," I'd blurted out. It was all I could think of to say. I wished I could take the experience away. I'd never meant to hurt him or Mama. To cause them this pain.

"Let's go home" was all he'd said before he turned and led the way out of the hospital to the parking lot.

I ran a hand over the stubble along my jaw. I felt unwashed, unshaven. I should have shaved, I thought, glancing at my father's clean profile as he drove. I wouldn't have been such an embarrassment to him at the hospital. I might have felt a little less pitiful, too. My eyes were dry and gritty from lack of sleep, my stomach was queasy, and I still felt hollow inside. I looked down at the book in my hand: *A Christmas Carol*. I don't know why but I carried the book around with me like a talisman. Maybe because it reminded me of a rare moment of connection with my brother. Maybe, too, because holding the book reminded me that I could find a way to break the ponderous chain I was dragging. And maybe because it helped me hope that I could survive my past and present to a better future.

Beside the book lay a bag of pills in my lap. So many different ones. I wondered if suicide wasn't easier.

I didn't know how they let me go home. The doctor asked me the same questions the three previous doctors had. I'd got a new prescription for depression, another to help me sleep, and a few others for God only knew what. If the pills kept the nightmares away, I didn't care what I took.

I squeezed my eyes shut. How was I going to make it? I was unfit company. They'd taught me the combat mind-set. How to look for threats, how to always be on alert, checking for dangers. They didn't teach us how to turn that off when we went home. I didn't know how to live not in war anymore.

I felt so alone. I didn't talk to anyone because no one understood what I was going through. Not family, not friends. I didn't blame them. I had a hard time talking to anyone now. And I didn't want to burden people with my problems. Marines were supposed to be tough. We were taught to suck it up. That we could get through anything, oo-rah! So to admit I had a problem, or worse, a disability, felt to me more than a failure. It was a betrayal.

It was dark when we arrived home. The holiday lights flickered merrily on Pinckney Street. We pulled up at the house. My mother had turned on the holiday lights, no doubt hoping to make me feel more cheery when I arrived home. Mama thought holiday decorations could cheer anyone up. But the blinking fairy lights and bright red bows had the opposite effect. They mocked how detached I felt from the joy of the season. I just wanted to get to my room, away from prying eyes. I didn't want to answer any more questions. I didn't want to join the family. I didn't want to live.

My father parked the car in the garage and let his hand rest on the steering wheel. We sat a moment in the dark. I waited. I felt he wanted to say something. But he opened his door and without a word returned to the house. I sat in the dark car a moment longer, clutching my bag of pills, and looked out in the darkness. *I should leave,* I thought. I'd move out after Christmas. I didn't want to put my family through any more heartache. I got out of the car and slammed the door, then walked with my head ducked into my collar and my hands in my pockets along the paved walk to the front door. Pushing open the door, I was hit by the heated, pine-scented air.

My mother stepped out from the kitchen into the front hall to greet me. She was wearing the same blue sweater over jeans, and her hair in the same hairstyle she'd worn since I was a child. She twisted a dish towel in her hands and her face was starched with an expectant smile. Miller stood behind her, sullenly staring. The fear I saw in his eyes nearly killed me.

"I'm sorry," I said in a rush, and went directly to the stairs. I was halfway up when I heard my mother call after me, "You got a phone call! A Clarissa Black from Pets for Vets. She said to call her as soon as possible."

I froze. My mother's words had permeated the

wall around me. They traveled deep inside my brain, past the stormy darkness swirling there to where one infinitesimally small flame of hope still flickered. *A dog,* I thought, and I felt that small flame surge. In all my despair I'd forgotten about the interview with Clarissa. I barely remembered it now. I gripped the stair railing and slowly turned to see my mother standing at the bottom of the stairs, her face uplifted, and waiting. Damn if I didn't see that flicker of hope in her eyes, as well.

"Thanks." Grasping at a straw, I replied, "I'll call her."

Two days later, I was sitting in an overstuffed chair in the living room, clean shaven, showered, wearing a freshly ironed shirt and polished shoes, waiting for my meeting with my dog. I took great care dressing for this meeting, as I would for any first date. After all, this was the beginning of a new relationship in my life, arguably one of the most important.

While in the hospital I'd met a guy who had a service dog, and he swore that dog saved his life. He told me how one night he had picked up the phone and was either going to call the suicide prevention hotline or Pets for Vets. He called Pets for Vets. I wasn't a doctor, but I knew I needed more help than I was getting from pills. So I took the card he gave me and when I was discharged from the hospital I applied for a service dog. Clarissa came out to my apartment to interview me a week later. She told me she needed to learn more about me, my personality, my wants and needs, to get a picture of the dog she would find for me in a shelter.

"Sort of like match.com?" I'd asked her.

She'd laughed but she didn't deny it.

"The way I look at it, you and the dog save each other. It's win-win."

Her questions were exhausting but thorough. I didn't care what the dog looked like—white, black, big, small, male, female. I just wanted a smart dog with a big heart.

So here I was, waiting for Clarissa's arrival, only this time she was coming with the dog she'd matched with me. I had my doubts she'd find the perfect dog for me. It seemed too good to be true that a dog could change my life. But I'd already tried so many different therapies. I was running out of options.

Clarissa had agreed to come today, Friday, so that Miller would be in school when the dog arrived. I was worried how Miller would react to my getting a dog. What with how much he pined for a dog of his own. Would he understand what a service dog was compared to a pet? Could he understand that I didn't just want this dog, I *needed* this dog? He was only ten years old. I didn't think he would.

The doorbell rang and my whole body tensed. I clenched my knees and forced myself to keep my feet planted on the floor and remain seated, which is what Clarissa had instructed me to do. Frommy chair I heard the door open, the high-pitched sound of greetings, then my mother and Clarissa sharing pleasantries. It was hard not to get up, but discipline prevailed. I counted to ten slowly, calming myself. A moment later my mother came in, her eyes glittering with excitement. She told me she was instructed to put the blindfold over my eyes. I knew this was part of the process. I could've just closed my eyes, but I went along with the blindfold. The idea was that when I opened my eyes, I'd have that first moment when I would see the dog up close, rather than watching the dog walk in. It was meant to be a wow moment.

Once the blindfold was secure, Mama called out the okay. "I'm leaving now. Clarissa said it was important you be alone." Mama kissed my cheek and I heard her retreating footfalls.

I could feel the tension mounting inside me. I sensed I was being watched. It took all my determination not to rip off the blindfold.

"Hi, Taylor," Clarissa called out as she walked in. Her voice was calm and cheery.

I imagined her the last time I saw her. Exceptionally pretty, blond, blue-eyed. You'd expect she was a model, not someone who trained service dogs. She was the kind of girl I'd normally ask out. But these were not normal times and Clarissa Black was all-business.

I cleared my throat. "Hey, Clarissa." With the blindfold on, my other senses were heightened. I heard the swish of jeans as she walked closer, smelled a floral scent and something else . . . something animal. I heard the command "Sit." Suddenly I sensed another presence close to me. With a shuffling Clarissa took a seat near me, then all went quiet.

Clarissa said in a formal tone, "Taylor, I'd like to present to you, in the name of Pets for Vets, this service dog to thank you for your service to your country." She paused and I heard the smile in her voice. "You can remove your blindfold."

I tore off the blindfold, and the first thing I saw were two large, soulful brown eyes staring straight into mine.

This was a big dog, bigger than I'd planned on. And formidable. His dense, short hair was as glistening a black as a raven's wing. He had the face of a Lab and the body of a smaller Great Dane. He looked to be a force of nature, a dog not to be messed with. Part of that impression came from his Great Dane size and black color, but also from the way he held himself, straight, confident, yet with an aloofness I admired. This was no goofball. I felt I could regain my own confidence with this dog.

Yet I didn't feel that willingness to touch yet. "He's a good-looking dog," I said stiffly, sitting erect and still with the same aloofness as the dog.

"His name is Thor." Clarissa reached out to stroke his long neck and broad back. Her face softened as she did so. "He was named that because of the white lightning bolt on his chest."

I checked that out, and his white chest markings did indeed look like a bolt of lightning. Thor, the God of Thunder. I liked that, too. I glanced up at Clarissa. She was watching both me and the dog intently. I knew she was looking for signals, trying to ascertain if she'd made a good match.

"We found Thor sitting in a shelter. He was on the list to be euthanized. He only had another day or two at most. When I saw him and looked into his eyes, I knew he was special. He passed the temperament evaluation form with flying colors. He might appear stoic, but he's actually very social."

It was hard to imagine that this beautiful dog could be euthanized. "He's cool," I said appraisingly.

She laughed. "Yeah, he's that. And so are you." She laughed again.

I gave her a look that back in the day might have been construed as flirtatious, but in these circumstances, it was all about friendship and depending on each other for honesty.

"Some dogs always want to be near the master.

In the same room, even in the same bed. Some dogs are more independent. They still want close companionship, but from time to time they want to have their own space. Thor is that kind of dog."

"Suits me."

"I thought it might." She chuckled in self-deprecation. "I spent many long hours choosing not just a good dog for you, but the right dog. Let me tell you, Thor is smart. He not only responds well to commands, but he intuits your needs. There will be times you won't even have to give him a command. He'll just know in advance what to do. That quality is rare."

She pet Thor again, scratching behind his ears. "He's truly a great dog. He deserves someone to love him. The way I look at it, humans failed him, not the other way around." She paused, and then looked at me. "You haven't petted him yet."

I nodded and frowned, self-conscious. I studied Thor's massive head, his floppy ears, his broad, muscular shoulders, his gleaming black coat. I liked the dog. He was beautiful and soulful, stoic and smart. What was not to like? But as with all things now, my emotions were bottled up. I hadn't touched another creature with affection in so long. I'd thought—hoped—seeing the dog would somehow open that part of me up.

"You know," she said, "from the moment he

walked into the room, Thor hasn't taken his eyes off of you."

"Really?" I leaned closer to Thor. A lot of emotion lurked behind those eyes. This dog was a lot like me, I realized. He'd been hurt. Betrayed. He held all his emotions in check. Like me, I figured he wouldn't take the chance. It was a stalemate.

Then, surprising me, Thor lifted his paw and put it firmly on my thigh. I felt the weight of it touch my heart.

Thor's generous gesture opened the floodgates of my emotions. This dog had showed more courage than I. This great, powerful, beautiful dog was willing to take a chance on *me*—a broken, depressed, lonely Marine. I took a long, shuddering breath. I didn't realize I'd been holding it. In fact, I'd been holding my breath for months, ever since the explosion.

I reached out to place my hand on Thor's broad head. Tentatively at first. The fur was short, stubbly, like my own hair. As I let my hand skim the fur from his head down his neck to his massive shoulders, I looked in his eyes. I could see pain deep in his brown eyes, shadows of his invisible wounds. I could also see the same flickering of hope that I felt sure he saw deep in my own eyes. The hope that I would save him as I hoped he would save me.

"He's my dog," I said with conviction, then

cleared my throat of the emotion choking me.

Clarissa beamed like a proud mother. I wondered how many times she had made this kind of match. How many lives she had saved.

"If you're ready," she said, "I'd like to spend some time to go over Thor's diet, health records, and to teach you basic training."

"Thanks. I appreciate that."

"No thanks necessary. You don't think I'd just drop off your dog and say good-bye? We want to ensure your success. Initially we'll spend time with basic commands, earning his trust. And you will learn to feel comfortable with Thor as a constant canine companion. You need to learn to understand and 'read' your dog, as he must learn your cues, too. The goal is to make you a solid team."

I nodded. That was what I wanted, too.

We cleared the furniture from the center of the room and began an hour's basic training. I'd never trained a dog before, never learned to give basic commands. When I made mistakes, Thor gave me a break and complied anyway. He knew the drill. A real smart dog, I thought, and was glad for it. Clarissa had to remind me to lavish praise on his successes. To pet him often. For the first time in months I enjoyed touching another living thing.

After an hour Clarissa determined we had mastered the basics. She presented me with the welcome box, a cornucopia filled with everything I could need—leashes, toys, bowls, food, nail clippers, brushes, beds—you name it.

"I know it's been an emotional day, and you two need time to hang out and bond. We can continue tomorrow." Her tone of finality signaled that she was leaving. "Is ten o'clock good for you?"

"Tomorrow?" I didn't expect another training session at home. There would be continuing group classes later, likely after the Christmas holiday.

"Absolutely. Training your dog to be a service dog is not something that can be done in a day, a weekend, or even in a month. It will be an ongoing process continuing for the whole life of the dog. However, the most intense training will be in these early days and weeks. Taylor, after this rush of excitement there will be days when you will feel you are not progressing, and in fact you may think the whole process is going backward. Keep in mind that these days are normal, as long as they only happen occasionally. Training requires consistent, daily effort."

She paused and looked at me square on. "If you don't have the time to do this, or you aren't willing to spend time working and practicing with your dog daily, a service dog may not be for you. A lot is expected of them, and they deserve the right care. Every day, without fail, he must be cared for. This means he'll need to be taken out several times a day, cleaned up after, fed a nutritious meal at least once a day. His ongoing training must be maintained, even improved. He'll need mental and physical exercise and stimulation, to be groomed when necessary. Basically treated as a living, breathing creature under your care. If that sounds like too much of a commitment of time, a companion dog may be a more appropriate choice."

"I've got nothing but time," I replied lightly.

She studied me with the same intensity Thor had earlier. "Taylor, see"—she paused—"it's not just the training. As smart as Thor is, he's in some ways like a child, dependent on you for his well-being. You're a team. Where you go, he goes. He's more than your dog. He's your partner. Your guide. Your best friend."

I realized what she was telling me. This was a lifelong commitment. A decision to deal with the ups and downs of a dog at my side day in and day out. I shouldn't, couldn't, take it lightly. I looked at Thor, sitting closer to Clarissa than to me, calmly waiting for his next command. I knew a sudden fear that she was having second thoughts. That she would take Thor away. At that moment I knew I couldn't let her do that.

I gave Thor the command to come. He trotted immediately to my side and sat, looking up at me patiently. I looked down at this great dog.

He quietly exuded a steadfast patience and a willingness to serve. If I would dare. We had work to do, sure. There would be mistakes. But we'd solve them together.

I put my hand on Thor's head and looked up at Clarissa. "I understand. My commitment is absolute. This is my dog."

She smiled and I could see she was convinced.

I almost smiled back, but at the moment I heard a high-pitched voice behind me.

"What's going on?"

I swung around to see Miller standing at the threshold, still in his parka, his cheeks ruddy from the cold, his backpack hanging from one arm. His eyes were wide under a shock of brown hair falling across his brow.

"*You* got a dog?"

But I am sure I have always thought of Christmas time, when it has come round—apart from the veneration due to its sacred name and origin, if anything belonging to it can be apart from that—as a good time; a kind, forgiving, charitable, pleasant time . . .

—*A Christmas Carol*

Chapter 15
Miller

"It isn't fair!" I shouted.

All the adults—Taylor, my mother, and some blond lady I never saw before—swung their heads to stare at me with surprise on their faces. They weren't expecting me. I'd finished my exam early—aced it. My attention was caught by the big dog when it stood up and took a step in front of Taylor, blocking him, his eyes on me.

I stared back at them, my hands in fists and bubbling over with rage and, most of all, hurt. They'd lied to me! Taylor got a dog! It was always Taylor getting the attention. Taylor the big war hero. Whatever Taylor wanted, Taylor got. No one cared what I wanted. We could afford a dog for Taylor but not for me? How could my mother be so mean? How could Taylor get a dog when I told him how much I wanted one?

My mother spoke first, in that tone she uses when she doesn't want me to get hurt. "Miller . . ."

I didn't give her time to speak. "It isn't fair!" I shouted at the top of my lungs. Dropping my backpack, I spun on my heel and ran from the room. I heard my mother following me. All I knew was I couldn't bear to see her or talk to her.

I had to get away from her and Taylor. I had to try to outrun the hurt clawing at my chest. So I ran.

I ran out the back door, around the house to the street, and there I just kept running. I felt tears streaming down my cheeks and I was sobbing out loud. Even as I ran, I thought to myself I'd never heard myself cry like that, like a baby, loud and deep, from my heart. But I couldn't stop it. It came bubbling out from some deep well that I'd been filling for weeks. My feet pounded the pavement, my arms punched the pace, tight-fisted and close to my body. At first I didn't know where I was going. I was running from something. But when I reached Pinckney Street and passed the shops, the fog in my mind cleared. My sobbing stopped and I could hear my footfalls pattering on the street and my breath keeping pace. I knew where I was going.

"Miller, how nice to see you." Mrs. Davidson smiled at me in surprise when she opened the door. I hadn't been to the house in a few weeks, not since my daddy told me I couldn't have Sandy. When she looked closer at my face, however, her smile wobbled some and she got that sad expression that told me she'd seen that I'd been crying.

"Can I see Sandy?"

Her face scrunched in worry. "I don't know if that's a good idea."

"Please. Just one more time?"

Her face softened and she smiled again. "Sure, okay." She opened wide the door. "You know where they are. I'll get Dill."

"Thank you, ma'am."

I passed her and ran into the back room. All the puppies were in a larger pen now, higher and wider. I couldn't believe how much bigger they'd gotten in just two weeks. They were cuter than ever, rolling and playing and nipping at each other. One was sweeter than the next. They all looked so bouncy and happy, I wanted to get in there and roll around with them, just bury my face in their fur and let them climb over me with their puppy breath until I felt better.

My eyes sought out the only golden pup in the litter. Sandy. I found him across the pen sitting alone, chewing on a stuffed toy. When I drew near the pen, I called his name. "Sandy!" He didn't even look up. I felt sad and disappointed. *Has he forgotten me already?* I wondered. I slipped out of my parka and opened the gate. I had to be careful because the puppies started jumping up on my legs. I walked to Sandy and sat beside him. Immediately two other puppies came over. They started tugging at my sleeve and sniffing me. Sandy had stopped chewing his toy and sat up, quietly looking at me. I saw a red ribbon around his neck, and I knew that meant he was sold. I wanted to cry right then and there.

"Come here, Sandy." I patted my lap.

In a bound, Sandy climbed into my lap and put his paws on my shoulders and began licking my face. I didn't cry then. I started laughing. He'd remembered me.

I had to face that this was the last time I could play with Sandy. I picked up a stuffed rabbit and wiggled it. Immediately Sandy pounced on it, grabbing a long ear. This was our favorite game. I made a soft growling noise. Sandy did, too, as we played tug-of-war.

A few minutes later Mrs. Davidson came into the room. "Miller?"

I turned my head to look over my shoulder. Sandy was chewing the toy contentedly with a victor's expression. I dreaded this moment. "Yes?"

"Honey, your mother's here. She wants you to come out to the car."

I looked back down at the puppy and drew him back in my lap for the last time. "I hope you get nice owners," I told him. "Maybe a kid who will love you as much as I do." I shook my head and sniffed. "No, that's not possible. Nobody could love you more than me." I bent low to press my face against his fur one last time. "Good-bye, Sandy." I gave him a kiss. I felt the tears coming, but Dill had come into the room with his mother and I couldn't let him see me cry. I gently moved the puppy from my lap and found my way around the other fur balls out the gate.

Mrs. Davidson was holding my coat. She looked near ready to cry.

"Thank you, Mrs. Davidson."

"Everything's going to be all right." She bent to kiss me.

I ducked my head and walked sullenly to the front door. My mother was standing there, looking as sad as I felt. "Come on, honey." She held out her arm to me.

I didn't want her touching me. Did she think I'd forgiven her so easily? I scowled and walked past her out the door.

"Thanks for calling me," Mama said to Mrs. Davidson.

"Call me later, Jenny," Mrs. Davidson said to Mama in an urgent tone.

I sat in the dark car in the front passenger seat. It was just above freezing, and Mama had kept the car running with the heater on. It was getting dark again and it was barely four o'clock. It seemed to me it was dark all the time lately. Mama came walking swiftly down the path to the car and slid in beside me. I looked out the window, giving her the cold shoulder.

"So we're back there again?"

I didn't reply. I was learning from Taylor.

Without another word, Mama put the car in gear and backed out the driveway. We drove in dark silence down the narrow road. The head-lights shone like twin flashlights. I looked up and saw the bare branches of the trees overhead. They looked like the ribs of a great whale. On Pinckney Street, Mama slowed, then came to a stop in front of T. W. Graham's. Even in the winter the restaurant had the sandwich-board sign with the large hand-painted word EAT on top.

Mama put the car in park, turned off the engine, and unbuckled her seat belt. "Come on. We're going to talk."

I stared out the windshield and clenched my teeth. "I don't want to."

"I didn't ask you if you wanted to. Let's go."

"No," I said stubbornly.

"Miller," she said in that tone she used when she wanted me to be reasonable. "I know you're hurt. I want to explain what's going on. I'd like it to be just between us. You and me."

That stung and I swung my head around to face her. "We're not a team. You lied to me. I don't want to talk to you." I turned away, slumped deeper in the seat, and dug my fists in my pocket.

"Look, Miller," my mother said with heat. "I'm about at the end of my rope. Everyone's treating me like I'm the villain. All I'm trying to do is make y'all happy!" she exclaimed, her voice rising. "And you now what? I'm tired! I'm tired of always trying and you always shutting me out. And your brother shutting me out."

“You got him a dog!” I cried out accusingly.

“No, I didn’t,” she shouted back.

I don’t know who was more surprised that she shouted. Me or her.

Mama took a breath and said in a calmer voice, “This is important, Miller. So stop being a baby, unbuckle your seat belt, and get yourself into that restaurant. We need to talk, hear?”

She’d used her no-nonsense tone and I knew she was really getting mad. Begrudgingly I unbuckled my seat belt and pushed open the car door. I slammed the door for good measure, then walked with my hands in my pockets and my collar up to the entrance of the restaurant. The door swung open and Mr. and Mrs. Thorvalson came out. Mrs. Thorvalson recognized me and smiled, her blue eyes bright.

“Well, hey there, Miller! What a surprise. How are you? Excited for Christmas?”

“I guess,” I lied, looking at my feet. She was always real nice to me and let me visit the sea-turtle hospital at the SC Aquarium where she worked. “I’m here with my mama.”

My mother walked up at just that moment, and she and Mrs. Thorvalson kissed in welcome. They talked a few minutes about Christmas plans, then Mama gave me a nudge to enter the restaurant.

Usually I liked coming to T. W. Graham’s. It was real cozy, with the wood booths and square tables. But mostly I liked all the stuff on the walls—paintings, surfboards, fishing nets and equipment, funny signs. It was old-timey. My daddy said it was the only game in town. Mama called it a shrine. We came here a lot to eat crabs and fish. Daddy sometimes came to hang out with the Old Captains, a group of former shrimp boat captains who reminisced about days gone by. It wasn't crowded now. A few of the Old Captains sat in one of the booths.

"Pick a booth," Mama said.

I did and slid into it, still scowling.

Miss Claudia came up to the table wearing an apron with a big, showy Christmas pin. She was the owner's wife and made the best pies anywhere. "Hey, Jenny," she called out as she approached. Her smile shifted to me. "Miller, nice to see you. Are you getting excited for Christmas?"

"Yes'm."

"What brings you in today? Christmas shopping, eh?"

"Just came for a chat," Mama replied in a cheery voice. "And maybe some of your pie. What do you want, Miller?" Mama's face was smiling but her eyes weren't.

"Nothing."

"I'll have the key lime pie and coffee," Mama said. When Miss Claudia left, Mama folded her hands on the table and leaned far forward to catch my eye. "You're just hurting yourself by not getting pie." When I didn't reply, she gave an exasperated sigh. "Miller, I know you think Taylor got a dog for Christmas. It might seem like that. Yes, he got a dog. Yes, it's Christmas. But, no, it's not a gift or something he got for Christmas."

Yeah, right, I thought to myself. *If it walks like a duck, quacks like a duck, it's a duck.*

Her coffee came so she stopped talking and smiled at Miss Claudia while the mug and cream were set before her. Mama moved the plate of key lime pie to the center of the table and passed me a fork. I didn't want to eat it but I couldn't resist. It was my favorite. I took a bite with a scowl. Across from me, Mama sipped her coffee, her eyes never leaving my face.

She set down her cup. "The dog's name is Thor," she began. "He's not a pet. He's a service dog. There's a big difference." She paused to make sure I was listening. When I looked up from my pie, she continued, "Taylor applied for this dog months ago, when he got out of the hospital. Thor is specially trained to help your brother with his PTSD. I've been reading about it and I've learned a lot. It's called post-traumatic stress disorder because it happens after a trauma. That means he got it from something terrible that happened to him in the war. Probably the IED explosion. He survived the blast, but his brain got hurt. Can you understand that? His injured brain makes him do these things we don't understand. Like how he's been staying in his room and doesn't go out. And how he gets angry all the time. And his bad nightmares?"

I nodded, listening now.

"Thor is trained to wake him up if he has those nightmares."

I looked at her with doubt; I didn't know whether to believe her. "Like, how?"

"When he has a nightmare, Thor will lick his hand and his face to wake him up before Taylor gets too deep into the dream. He can sense when it's happening. The same for when he starts to get angry or anxious."

I shrugged.

"Do you remember how you said Taylor wasn't the same person? How you didn't like who he was now?"

I looked away. "Yeah."

"Me, too. I'm ashamed I thought that. Are you?"

I felt choked up and nodded.

Mama reached out to pat my hand. "It's okay. Here's the thing. A service dog is a kind of therapy for Taylor. I hope . . . I pray . . . that Thor will help Taylor get back to being the guy we love. Taylor only got the phone call the other day that his dog was ready. He'd been waiting for months. Honey, he didn't get a dog as a Christmas gift. It was a coincidence that it was today so close to Christmas. Try to understand, Thor isn't a pet. Taylor needs this dog."

"Well, I need Sandy, too!" I cried back. "Why is it that what Taylor needs is more important than what I need? Who is going to feed Taylor's new dog, huh? He doesn't get up in the morning. And how can we afford to feed him and not Sandy?" I sniffed and wiped my nose with my sleeve. "It doesn't matter now, Sandy is sold and I can never have him. And that's not fair."

I shoved the plate of pie away and climbed from the booth. "I'm going home."

"Wait, I have to pay."

"I don't want to go with you. I'm walking."

As I opened the door, the bells chimed and Miss Claudia called out, "Merry Christmas!"

Yeah, right, I thought, blinking tears from my eyes. Walking home, when I saw the red ribbons and bows on the windows and doors, it made me feel sadder. All I could think of was the red "sold" ribbon around Sandy's neck.

The sight of these poor revelers appeared to interest the Spirit very much, for he stood with Scrooge beside him in a baker's doorway, and taking off the covers as their bearer's passed, sprinkled incense on their dinners from his torch.

—*A Christmas Carol*

Chapter 16
Jenny

Once again the doors were shut upstairs. I swear, all I wanted for Christmas was a normal, happy home without closed doors! Where was the season of brotherly love? I wondered. Those two brothers were not even talking. I was beginning to side with Team Scrooge.

I stood in the front hall still in my winter coat. It was after five but it felt like midnight. I was tired and drained. As I took my coat off, I realized the last thing I wanted to do was prepare a dinner for this crew. All I wanted to do was climb into bed and cry.

But of course I couldn't do that. I was the mother. At times like these, when I was at my wit's end, I brought to mind what Mother had told me the day I first held in my arms my newborn baby:

"Motherhood is your greatest joy and also your greatest challenge. From this day forward your life is no longer just your own. Mothers give, give, give, and when they think they have nothing left, they dig deep and give some more. Because a mother is the heart of a family. A family is only as happy as the mother."

Christmas was a week away. If I gave up now, what hope would my children have for any joy this holiday? I wouldn't be happy this Christmas if they were not. So I did as my mother advised and dug deep. I found my strength in remembering Christmases past when the boys were young. The excitement in their eyes when they helped make holiday cookies or went out to find a tree. Helping put out the nativity scene at our church. Hanging up stockings and leaving cookies for Santa. Visualizing their smiles, I felt a renewed energy.

With resolve bubbling inside my heart I turned on the radio to the Christmas station. The children made fun of me for playing the carols all throughout the holiday, but I believed it lifted the spirits—at least mine. Appropriately, the crooning of "It's the Most Wonderful Time of the Year" filled the room. I indulged myself and poured a glass of sherry. Sipping its sweetness, I went to the kitchen and scrounged my fridge to see what I had. I pulled out butter, bread, and cheddar cheese and began to make grilled-cheese sandwiches. It was comfort food in my book and perfect for a wintry night when the larder was low. As the cheese melted, I made up a few trays, decorating them with a holiday placemat and napkin. When the bread was golden and oozing cheese, I put the warm sandwiches on plates with chips, crisp carrots, and a few almond cookies. It wasn't a grand dinner but it made for a tasty supper.

First I carried a tray to Miller's room. I knocked and entered, finding Miller sitting on his bed sullenly reading Dickens.

"I'm not hungry," he said when he saw the tray.

"Uh-huh," I replied in good cheer. "It's here in case you change your mind." I left without another word, closing the door behind me. If I knew my son, that tray would be clean in an hour.

The second tray I carried to Taylor's room. I knocked and opened the door, not waiting for his usual "Go away." Unlike before, there was obviously some attempt at tidying the room. The dirty dishes and clothes were gone, as was the bottle of bourbon on the bedside table. I knew he'd cleaned up for Clarissa's inspection and hoped he'd keep it up. Taylor had always been a neat young man.

Taylor was sitting on the floor with Thor's head in his lap reading a book. My heart melted at the sight. *A boy and his dog,* I thought. Yet I knew something more important was going on. I could see Taylor was pensive.

"I thought Thor left with Clarissa?"

"Why would you think that? Thor's my dog now. He stays here. Clarissa comes back only to train."

"Oh." I was glad to hear it. Already I could see the dog was having a positive effect on Taylor.

"I thought we could all use some quiet time tonight." I swept into the room, carrying the tray to his desk. My prying eyes noticed the pamphlets and books on dog training scattered.

"What are you reading?"

"*A Christmas Carol*."

"Oh, really? Miller is reading that for his book report."

"I know. I thought I might be able to help him." Taylor closed the book abruptly and moved it aside, seemingly embarrassed. "Or not." He stroked Thor's long neck in thought. "How's Miller?"

I set down the tray and turned to face Taylor. "As you'd expect," I replied honestly. "Hurt."

"I can understand those feelings." Then in a lower tone he added, "I feel terrible about this."

"You shouldn't."

He let his arm drop from Thor. "How can I not? I got a dog and he didn't. That's a kick in the teeth for anyone, much less a kid only ten years old." He paused. "You know"—Taylor rubbed his forehead with his fingers—"he told me how much he wanted that dog. I wanted to get it for him. Real bad. I walked to Mrs. Davidson's house that same day to buy it. But she told me the dog was already sold. All the puppies were all sold."

I was stunned that he'd walked all the way across town to the Davidsons' house. Taylor, who never left the house. "You should tell Miller that."

"Why? What good would it do? It'd only rub salt in the wound. Too little, too late. Damn, this is such a mess."

Thor heard Taylor's tension, and I was mightily impressed to see the dog immediately rise and turn to bring his face to Taylor's and begin licking it. Taylor had to stop talking and began petting Thor, murmuring, "It's all right. Good dog."

I watched, for the first time understanding the remarkable sensitivity of the service dog. Thor really could sense Taylor's anxiety levels and calm him before they went out of control. Taylor wasn't even fully aware that he'd stopped to focus on petting the dog.

"Taylor, you can't take blame for the fact you got a dog," I told him. "Just like you can't take blame for what's happened in Afghanistan."

"Daddy thinks I deserve the blame."

"What? How can you say that?"

"He hasn't spoken a word to me since, since . . ." Taylor paused and looked away. He didn't need to mention the incident with the gun. We were both thinking of it. "He can't stand to even look at me."

I licked my lips, unsure of what to say. I'd noticed Alistair's avoidance, too. "He's just so worried about getting his job done," I said lamely.

"Whatever." Taylor shook his head.

My heart broke for him and I resolved to talk to Alistair when he returned home.

"Here's the thing," Taylor said. "I can't keep the dog."

"What?" I asked with alarm.

"At least not while I'm here. It'd be too hard for Miller. He's the one we have to worry about. Not me."

"I'll be the judge of who I worry about, thank you very much."

Taylor furrowed his brows, intent on saying his piece. "I can call Clarissa," he said, pushing forward with his thoughts. "I'll ask if she'll take Thor back, just until after Christmas. Then I can find a new place."

I didn't like where these plans were heading. Give back the dog? Leave home after Christmas? "A new place?" I asked. "Taylor, where will you go?"

"I'm not going back to Quantico. I left that hellhole of an apartment. It was only temporary. I want to find someplace that's good for Thor. And for me."

"You know you can stay here for as long as you want. We want you to. This is your home."

He bowed his head. "I know. Thanks." He looked back up. "But I can't keep Thor and live here under these circumstances. The last thing I want to do is hurt Miller."

I saw the decision forming in his mind and feared it. This was the Taylor I knew and loved. He put others before himself. Self-sacrifice and a strong sense of duty were some of the reasons he'd joined the Marines. I could already see the calming effect the dog was having on my son. I couldn't let him make this mistake.

"I almost lost you and I won't do it again." Emotion made my voice wobble. "I know you're having a hard time. I want to help in any way I can, to help you deal with your condition now that I understand it better. . . . Yeah," I said self-consciously when he appeared surprised. "I studied up on PTSD. There's so much information out there. Academic and lay. Even I could understand it," I added with a self-deprecating laugh. "And I know now that you need that service dog."

Taylor looked at the dog, then reached out to scratch behind Thor's ears.

I knew he was listening so I pressed on. "But we can do better as a family, I know we can. Even if it just means bringing you a grilled cheese sandwich in your room instead of having you join us at the table." I met his gaze and smiled. "I know it's going to take time. I want to help you get your life back, and I know that includes your relationship with your brother and father. Give us time, Taylor. We *will* get through this and be a family again."

Taylor looked at his hands.

I saw his struggle and sighed. One of the things I'd learned was to be patient. Not to pressure him into talking. And to stay positive. "Don't make any decisions tonight. The dog is here. You've already begun to bond. If you give him back now, what message are you giving to *him?* Rejection? He might not trust you again."

Taylor didn't respond, but his brows furrowed, and he looked at Thor, petting his fur. I admired how the dog stayed right by his side, sensing Taylor needed him.

"I have a suggestion. Tonight, keep your door open. That way, when Miller goes to the bathroom, he won't be able to help himself but take a peek at the dog. There's never been a dog he didn't love. Once he accepts Thor . . ."

"If."

I shrugged. "If . . . Maybe that will break the ice between you and then you can talk. Help him to understand why you got Thor. This is going to be touchy any way you look at it, for both of you. Let's try and take each day as it comes."

Taylor nodded in agreement. "Okay. I'll try anything. He's my kid brother." Taylor's voice broke. "I haven't been very nice to him lately. I know that." He looked up at me from the floor and our eyes met. I was stunned to see his were watery. "But I love him."

He went to church, and walked about the streets, and watched the people hurrying to and fro, and patted children on the head, and questioned beggars, and looked down into the kitchens of houses, and up to the windows, and found that everything could yield him pleasure. He had never dreamed that any walk—that anything—could give him so much happiness.

—*A Christmas Carol*

Chapter 17
Taylor

The following morning I awoke feeling a little disoriented. Oddly rested. I blinked hard to pull myself from my sleepy stupor and turned my head toward the window. The curtains were drawn but shafts of bright white light broke through the borders, telling me the sun was already rising. I shifted my gaze to the bedside table and grabbed my phone. I couldn't believe it was almost 8:00 a.m. I'd slept for six hours! I couldn't remember the last time I'd slept so long. I ran my hand over my head. It had to be Thor. The dog was the reason I could sleep for the first time in months—because I felt safe.

Remembering the dog, I turned on my side and rose up on my elbow to peer over the mattress to his dog bed on the floor. I couldn't believe what I saw and stifled my laugh of surprise. On the floor in the enormous dog bed I saw Miller sleeping with his arm around Thor's neck. My frozen heart cracked.

I quietly, carefully, snapped a photo with my phone. I didn't think anyone would believe me if I told them. It was the very image of innocence. I wanted to remember this moment always, to look at it when I needed something good to hold on to. Lowering the phone, I thought of my mother and her wise advice. She'd always been there for me. Even when I was at my worst. She made me want to be a better son.

I rose to sit. Immediately Thor reacted and climbed to his feet to check on me. I felt the intensity of those dark brown eyes searching my face. I reached out to pat his head.

"I'm okay, boy," I told Thor with a fond chuckle at the spectacle of Miller's having been tossed and awakened on the floor.

Miller sat up and rubbed his eyes while yawning.

"You must be freezing." He wore socks, but he'd slept on the floor without a blanket.

"I'm okay. Thor kept me warm."

"So . . . you like him?"

Miller nodded. "Yeah." He released a reluctant smile as he reached out to pet the big dog's back. He was rewarded with a sloppy kiss from Thor.

"He likes you."

"Yeah."

I caught Miller's grin. I rubbed my palms together and gathered my thoughts. "I didn't intend to get him before Christmas. I know how much you wanted that puppy. The timing just worked out this way."

Miller kept his gaze on Thor as he continued to stroke his back. He didn't respond.

"You see, Thor is specially trained to help me with my PTSD."

"I know," Miller said in a monotone. "Mama explained all that to me."

I looked at his hurt expression. "But that doesn't really matter, does it? You still didn't get a dog. It still isn't fair, is it?"

Miller tightened his lips and shook his head.

I exhaled a long breath, making my decision. "I didn't think so. So, I've been thinking. I have a responsibility to the dog. And the dog has a responsibility to me. I can't give you Thor. But I also have a responsibility to you. My brother. Now," I continued, "there are rules on how to behave with service dogs we must follow. But I was wondering if you would help me take care of Thor. If you would be his friend."

Miller swung his head up to look at me. "What? Sure!" He leaped up and hugged me tight. "You're the best brother ever," he choked out.

I hugged him tight, not feeling the least bit nervous or uncomfortable with the touch. After another tight squeeze I released him. Miller slid back to the floor and began petting Thor with a proprietary relish.

"He's a great dog." Miller beamed. "When I came in last night, he came right up to me and sniffed me. Then he licked my face. Right off the bat. That's a good dog, right?"

"He's the best."

Miller pet Thor a while longer, lost in thought. “So, we’ll both take care of him?” he asked, wanting to be sure he got it right.

“He’s big enough for two.”

Miller laughed at that. “Yeah, he sure is.”

“There is a lot to do,” I said, warming to the idea. “Feeding twice a day, walking him, grooming him. And of course, the training. Oh, about that,” I said, thinking of Clarissa. She would not allow Miller to train in class. “Since he’s a service dog, I’ll have to do the formal training in class.”

“No problem. I get it.”

This is a good start, I thought, taking heart. I was talking to my brother again. I knew he loved me. But I had a ways to go before earning back his pride.

Never underestimate the value of good sleep. I was more focused, less angry, and willing to get out of my room. Things went smoothly the next few days as Miller, Thor, and I fell into a routine. We fed and groomed the dog together. Most significant, we also took Thor for walks together. These were important forays for me out of the house. I recalled what Clarissa had said about Thor needing his own time. When Miller and I took him out in the woods, we stopped at an open field and released his leash. Thor ran the length of the field, relishing his freedom. The air was crisp and the sky was clear. The wind had a bite so we pulled up our hoods over our ears as we watched our dog prance like a racehorse. When I called him back, he returned with speed, moist from the exertion but with what Miller and I agreed was a grin.

On the third day the sky continued to be clear. It was colder so we wore hats and gloves and scarves and decided to walk into town to do a little Christmas shopping. All in all, our outings were going pretty good. A big step for me and proof of how Thor was helping me get up and out. I hadn't purchased gifts for anyone, and neither had Miller, he'd confessed. Christmas was just around the corner. Miller and I compiled our lists and took off with Thor at our sides. It was late afternoon and already a sienna sunset streaked the sky.

"We're the Three Musketeers," Miller said, patting Thor.

"More like the Three Stooges," I quipped, and was pleased to hear Miller guffaw.

McClellanville wasn't a big city and there weren't crowds to navigate—two triggers for me. With only a few modest shops it was a perfect choice for my first outing in public with a service dog. Still, we would confront strangers and possible congestion on the sidewalk. Thor sensed my apprehension and walked close to my side, looking up at me frequently. I held the leash tight in my fist as we approached the shops along Pinckney Street. With Thor at my side my mind didn't panic, but I was feeling the tension mount. I was usually hypervigilant, checking over my shoulder or the tops of buildings, looking for snipers. Thor kept me in the moment as we walked. I knew he had my back. Plus, I had to think about him, where he was, and where Miller was.

The village was all decked out for the holiday. Some of the great old houses, white grandes dames with double porches, shone nostalgic with graceful boughs of greenery encircled with red ribbon draped between the pillars. White electric candles flickered in the windows. As we walked by, Miller and I looked at all the different decorations, some simple and natural, some wildly imaginative and electric. Every door held a wreath. The excitement in the air was contagious. Christmas was suddenly becoming real to me.

One couple stopped to admire Thor. Even though he had his service dog vest, they reached out to pet him. Clarissa had pounded into my head not to let people touch the dog. Especially not in the early few weeks of training. I wanted to tell them to stop, explain that my dog was working. People should ask permission to pet any dog, but especially a service dog. But this being my first time out with him, I felt tongue-tied. I didn't know the words to say, didn't want conflict, so I kept silent. Miller didn't help, either. He was by nature gregarious and enjoyed telling the strangers the dog's name, beaming with pride. To his credit, Thor bore it all with his usual aloof calm, neither licking the strangers nor fawning. I was proud of him. After we moved on, I knelt down beside him to praise him and give him a treat. Next, I explained the service dog protocol to Miller.

It was a good lesson to learn for all of us. Feeling buoyed with confidence, we went on to the first shop. The cute pink cottage was filled with handmade, handcrafted items.

"I'm sure we can find something for Mama in here," I said to Miller. I knew I had the right to go into the store with my service dog, so, taking a breath, I pushed open the windowpaned door swathed in a bough of pine. A small bell tinkled as we stepped inside, where it smelled of cinnamon and pine. It was a sweet shop, feminine, with a decorated Christmas tree, lights everywhere, and jammed with a potpourri of gift items. The shopgirl, a pretty brunette wearing a red-and-green apron, looked up from the counter with a smile, then, seeing the dog, her smile faltered.

"I'm sorry, but no dogs allowed inside."

"It's my service dog," I replied, standing awkwardly at the door.

She looked puzzled. "I still don't think it's allowed."

I could feel the tension building in my gut. “It is,” I told her through clenched teeth. “It’s the law.”

Worry flickered across her face. “I . . . I don’t know. I have to check. Can you wait a moment, please?” She hurried to the back room.

I could feel my temples begin to throb. Thor stood beside me, calm and patient, awaiting my next command. I removed my gloves and stroked his velvety fur and ears, finding comfort there.

The three other people in the shop turned around to openly stare at us. I didn’t like being the center of attention and my tension mounted. I could feel sweat pooling. Miller shifted his weight and grew uneasy. “Come on, Taylor,” he said in a low voice. “We don’t have to go in here.”

“Yes, we do,” I ground out. This was our test. Clarissa had warned me there would be times like this, and I had to remain calm but firm.

A moment later the shopgirl returned with an older woman, probably the owner. She, too, wore a red-and-green apron. She came around the counter and approached with a smile, but her sharp eyes were taking in the situation.

“Hello there,” she said cheerily. “You say this is your service dog?”

“He is.”

She looked at Thor’s red-and-black service vest, which was clearly marked SERVICE DOG.

"You don't look like you have a disability," she said, eyeing me.

"I didn't know there was a look," I replied without humor.

My tone was having a negative effect on the woman. "You know, a lot of people are faking those vests these days."

A couple in the store leaned toward each other and whispered.

I felt my cheeks flame. "Are they?"

"Yes. You're not blind. I don't see your injury." Her tone was getting hostile.

Miller was getting agitated. He spoke up on my behalf. "He's got PTSD."

I cringed. I didn't feel I had to give my name, rank, and diagnosis.

Suddenly, understanding flooded the shop woman's face. "Oh, my, you're the McClellan boy, aren't you? For heaven's sake, why didn't you say so? Come on in. I'm sorry to make you wait. We're so glad you're back home! Why, we just love your mama." She shuffled me into the store. "Oh," she added in a serious tone, "we thank you for your service."

My hands were shaking and my headache pounded. All I wanted to do was get out of the shop and gulp deep breaths of fresh air. But I forced a smile and shook her outstretched hand. "Thank you," I replied.

The three other people in the store were

McClellanville residents. They smiled sweetly and came forward to introduce themselves, all thanking me for my service.

I nodded, mumbling my thanks.

One woman reached out to pet Thor, but her companion, an elderly man, stopped her, putting his hand on her arm. "You should ask if you can pet his dog."

She looked up at me with embarrassment, pulling back her hand. "Oh. Sorry!"

"He's a service dog," I told her. "He shouldn't be distracted."

The woman nodded quickly and with a wobbly smile escaped behind a wall of pottery.

I sighed and wanted to leave, but Miller was busily looking at more pottery across the store. When he looked up, he waved me over excitedly. Walking through the narrow aisles, all I could think about was Thor's mighty tail sweeping off the contents of a lower shelf with one swish.

"I think Mama will like this," Miller said, showing me a small hand-painted dish meant to hold a spoon on the stove. His eyes sought my approval.

I basked in his gaze and took his quest seriously. I checked the price and it was appropriately low, something he could afford. "It's perfect." I looked at the array of matching pottery dishes in the set. They were cream colored, trimmed in red, shellfish themes, notably crabs and shrimp. "I'll get the matching casserole dish."

"That's great!" Miller was thrilled that we were giving something together.

When I saw the doggy bow ties in Christmas motifs, I bought one for Thor while Miller hooted. We gathered our items and checked out. The now overly friendly shopgirl offered to wrap the presents, which we were both grateful for. I had two left thumbs when it came to wrapping presents and I was out of practice. She used gold paper printed with holly berries and tied it with glittery gold ribbon. Thanking her profusely, we moved on.

Outside the store, Miller and I looked at each other and laughed. It was a great release.

"I thought for sure I'd be buying a bag full of broken glass and pottery," I said.

"Yeah." Miller laughed. "Thor barely made it through the aisles."

We passed a few women's clothing shops with beautiful sweaters and scarves in holiday colors. I gazed at a creamy cashmere sweater in red and thought my mother would look beautiful in it with her dark hair. But alas, I'd already purchased the casserole dish and moved on.

I thought I could handle one more shop. We went next to the Arts Council, where historic and handcrafted items were for sale. Peeking in the window, I could see no one else was inside. I don't know if word had spread or with its being a public building they were educated in the laws concerning service dogs, but we didn't have any trouble entering. Relieved, I left Miller in the shop and sauntered over to the adjoining gallery, where paintings by local artists were on exhibit. I'd always enjoyed art and thought someday I'd try my hand at it. I wasn't a van Gogh or anything, but I'd done some art therapy in the hospital and enjoyed it. I wasn't too bad at it, either. A lot of talent was on the walls, I thought as I strolled past. Thor was at ease in the large, empty room, keeping his gait even with mine. I stopped before one painting, an oil on canvas that depicted a few shrimp trawlers at dock. The sky was a vivid blue with white cumulus clouds, and great green nets hung from the rigging like folded butterfly wings. The artwork was masterful, but what struck me was the name on one of the boats. The *Miss Jenny*. I felt a sudden stab of wanting. I glanced at the small white card to the lower right of the painting. I didn't know the artist and the price was reasonable for an oil, but still out of my means. Yet I continued to study the small painting for some time.

"I found something for Dad," Miller called from the entrance to the gallery. He had a book in his hand.

I dragged my attention away from the painting. Thor and I walked out of the gallery back to the shop to inspect. It was a history book about McClellanville, complete with photographs.

"Dad likes history," Miller said.

The salesman overheard us. "That's a new one. Just came out this year. And you can return it if he already has it or doesn't like it."

"He'll like it," I assured Miller, and knew our father would never return Miller's gift even if he did have a copy.

I was getting weary and ready to head back. It was the longest I'd stayed out for weeks. I browsed through the store looking for something for my father. I didn't have much time left to shop. There were photographs of old McClellanville he might like, a few woolen scarves that he would never wear, jewelry he'd put in a drawer. The painting was niggling my thoughts, calling me back. I guided Thor back into the gallery and went directly to the painting of the shrimp boats. Damn, but I liked it better now than before. It spoke to me and I knew my father would not just like it—he would love it. I could visualize it hanging over his desk in his office.

"Wow," Miller exclaimed at my side. "It's the *Miss Jenny*! You've got to get it! How much is it?"

"A lot. At that price, it's an investment." Then deciding, I reached out to lift the painting from the wall. It was heavy with the driftwood frame, a nice heft to go with the price. "But worth every penny."

As I carried it to the counter, I felt enveloped in the spirit of Christmas.

"Oh, that's a nice one," the salesman commented. "A lot of people have had their eye on it. To the swift goes the race, eh?" He winked.

I watched with confidence in my purchase rising as the salesman wrapped the painting in thick brown paper. The old saying *It's better to give than to receive* never rang more true than it did now.

"Dad's going to flip out when he sees that," Miller said. I knew he felt a sense of ownership by virtue of taking part in the decision to buy it. "It kinda goes with my present, too," he added with authority.

"Yep." I bought some wrapping paper, ribbon, and cards. Miller picked out a few craft ornaments that would appeal to our mother. With that, we were done. Or almost.

"I still have to get you something," I said.

"You got me something already. Thor!" Miller reached out to stroke the dog's head.

Thor took the moment to lie on the floor by our feet. He was so big and took up so much floor space, I thought it was a good thing no one else was in the shop.

"I can't wrap him up with a bow on Christmas morning. What else do you want?"

Miller shrugged and looked away. "Nothing."

I saw the swift shift in emotion and knew that

he was thinking of his puppy, Sandy. There was nothing I could say so we remained quiet, waiting for our packages to be tallied and bagged. I pulled my wallet from my pants pocket and paid the bill.

We left the shop calling out our thanks. I still had to get something for Miller, but the sky was already darkening. It had been a long day for Thor, and Miller and I were both eager to get to our rooms and hide our treasures.

Suddenly a car backfired. I plunged into a crouching position with my back against a brick wall. I was back in the war, my eyes wildly searching the roofs of buildings, my heart pounding in my ears. My blood raced and the whole world started spinning. I swung my head from left to right in a panic, seeing my Marine brothers' faces, hearing explosions in my head.

A sound. A feeling. Moist. Comforting. It took me a minute but gradually I processed that it was Thor's licking my face, whimpering in worry. His paws were on either side of my legs, his chest braced against me as he stood guard over me. Slowly I realized where I was and my breathing returned to normal. After a few minutes my hand was still shaking but I could move it.

"Good dog." I reached out to pet Thor. I took a few more deep breaths, then moved him a few steps back from me and felt the wintry air enter the space. I gulped mouthfuls of it.

"Are you okay?"

I looked up to see Miller standing near, watching me with those fearful eyes again. I felt a stab of disappointment. He clearly didn't know what to do with his crazy brother crouched on the sidewalk. Nor did I. I thought I'd been doing so well, and *bam!* One loud noise and I was back in Afghanistan. I was a walking powder keg.

A couple walked past me, looking over their shoulders with suspicion.

With a hefty grunt I rose to my feet, using Thor's strong back as support. Then I leaned against the building while my nerves settled. I was still shaking and dizzy. Meanwhile Miller went about collecting my packages.

"How's the painting?" I was worried I'd torn it.

"Feels okay." He shrugged.

"Good." I felt embarrassed. I looked at my feet. "Sorry I freaked out."

"It's okay."

I sighed and met his gaze. "No. It isn't okay. But I have to deal with it."

"Yeah. It's that PTSD, right?"

My brows rose. "Right." In truth, it was nice to talk about it with his knowing the facts about the disorder and accepting it.

"I thought Thor was supposed to make that go away."

"He's trying." I patted the dog's great head. Thor was still watching me intently, worry shining in his beautiful eyes. "But it takes time. I mean, without Thor I'd never have come with you to town. I'd still be hiding out in my room. Hell, without Thor I'd still be a shivering mess on the street."

I tried to make a joke of it and looked at Miller. His blue eyes, barely visible beneath his fringe of brown hair smashed down on his forehead by his knit cap, were serious. He was mulling over what I'd said. That wasn't disgust I saw in his eyes. It was sadness. For me and my troubles, I realized with a pang of affection. I was humbled and thought I was damn lucky to have such a brother.

"What do you say we go home?"

Miller was more than willing.

Without further stops we made our way home through the small village, a man, a boy, and a dog, past houses now aglow with holiday colors, a biting breeze at our faces, our arms filled with our purchases. I looked down at Thor, walking by my side, nose in the air, alert. He was working. I understood now what my Marine brother in the hospital meant when he'd said his dog had changed his life. All the reports I'd read online from servicemen with PTSD claiming their dog had helped them rebuild their fractured lives I now knew were true. I'd tried so many different therapies, but it was this dog, Thor, who gave me back hope for a normal life.

"If I could work my will," said Scrooge indignantly, "every idiot who goes about with 'Merry Christmas' on his lips, should be boiled with his own pudding, and buried with a stake of holly through his heart. He should!"

—*A Christmas Carol*

Chapter 18
Taylor

With the shopping expedition under my belt, on the twenty-third we tackled the next outing—the high school play. Miller had just begun his Christmas vacation and complained that it was grossly unfair that he had to go see a school play, but it was *A Christmas Carol* and for extra credit he obliged, putting on his thick corduroy pants, a navy sweater, and his new boots. I teased him that if I could go to the play with my PTSD, he had to man up and go, too. It was good to talk openly about my PTSD. It didn't feel any longer like some dirty secret I had to hide behind a closed door.

Unspoken, however, was a strange new bond we'd formed over the book, *A Christmas Carol*. Knowing we were both reading it, we frequently checked on each other's reactions to different scenes or carried on a running debate about which ghost was the best. I preferred the Ghost of Christmas Past—the distant past. I found comfort remembering times when I was as young and carefree as Ebenezer was when he'd danced with the pretty ladies at Fezziwig's party. Miller was behind the Ghost of Christmas Present. The ghost's feast cinched it for him: *turkeys, geese, game, poultry, prawn, great joints of meat, sucking-pigs, long wreaths of sausages, mince-pies, plum-puddings, barrels of oysters, red-hot chestnuts, cherry-cheeked apples, juicy oranges, luscious pears, immense twelfth-cakes, and seething bowls of punch*. But also because he liked Tiny Tim. That gentle-hearted character had a lot in common with my little brother.

I put on my best jacket and a freshly ironed shirt. Thor had a good brushing and his fur was gleaming. Mama wore her best red wool dress, which set off her cap of chestnut hair, and the green silk scarf decorated with holly that she'd received from Daddy several Christmases ago. She always brought it out for the holiday parties. Mama never wore much makeup. She didn't need to. Even with all the extra hours of work she'd taken on this past week, her green eyes glittered with the expectation of a night out. I thought she'd never looked more beautiful. Daddy was unable to join us because he was once again working late, getting a house job finished by the Christmas Eve deadline. I had to respect him for that.

When I came downstairs, I paused at the landing to sniff the air. Ecstasy! Mama had a pork roast in the slow cooker, and the delectable scents of garlic and rosemary permeated the house. I knew there'd be roasted potatoes, too.

My stomach growled. Thor gave me a piteous glance, then turned to the kitchen, clearly wanting to head in that direction.

"Soon, pal." I stroked his fur.

We put on our winter coats, gloves, and scarves and loaded into Mama's car for the short drive to Lincoln High School. I went to this high school years ago, and from the outside, it looked exactly the same. We piled out of the car and waited in line at the front entrance, where a few students were collecting tickets.

A young girl of about seventeen looked at Thor, then at me, with a worried expression. *Here we go again,* I thought, and felt my stomach tighten.

But this time Mama stepped to the front. "Merry Christmas, Melissa," she said in a friendly yet firm voice. "Have you met my son Taylor? He's a Marine," she said with pride. "And that's his service dog. I'm sure you know it's the law that people with service dogs can go anywhere, right? Yes, I'm sure you do. Now here are our tickets. Thank you. And Merry Christmas!" Mama concluded with a cheery wave and led us all past the stunned girl at the door into the school auditorium.

"Mama would make a great drill sergeant," I said to Miller as we followed her in.

I gawked like a tourist as I followed my mother through the halls that I would have been able to navigate in my sleep. I'd spent four of the happiest years of my life in these halls. It seemed like a lifetime ago since I was that kid who didn't have a care in the world. How much had changed since then, I thought. How much I had changed.

"Hey, Taylor!" came a shout from across the hall. Thor sensed me startle and stood in front of me, blocking.

It was Jack, my old friend. He was wearing the lowcountry man's uniform of tan Dockers pants and a navy blazer. I nodded and waved. I was getting more comfortable being out in public with Thor, but I wasn't ready to start talking at length with anyone.

The school band mercifully began making noises.

Mama said, "We'd better hurry and get some seats."

"I'll call you again after Christmas," Jack shouted with a parting wave as he guided a petite blonde carrying an infant past the double doors.

We found seats in the back which allowed Thor to sit in the aisle. Miller wanted to sit by him and hold his leash, but I held firm. I needed Thor tonight. I didn't want to make a mistake and cause a scene or have Thor bark and interrupt the play. As the curtain went down and the room darkened, I clutched the arms of my seat and knew a moment's panic. But when I felt Thor's muzzle on my knee, I took a deep breath and began petting him repeatedly. The dog and I were connected at an almost cellular level. Thor could sense my needs and I his. I was beginning to understand what Clarissa meant when she said the leash was more an umbilical cord. Thor had faith in us. I needed to have faith, too.

I relaxed more and enjoyed the program. I didn't hear a peep from Thor. He could've been asleep for all we were aware. The young players did an admirable job with their roles, especially old Jacob Marley when he rattled his chains and moaned for the soul of old Scrooge. I nudged Miller in the ribs when we heard the familiar lines, and he glanced back at me with a smirk. He'd received an A on his book report. I wished our father could have joined us. He always enjoyed these special family occasions. And I wanted him to be proud to see me getting out more.

When we drove home, we were all hungry and in good moods. The night had been a success on many levels. As usual, Mama turned on the station that only played Christmas carols. This time I didn't mind. When we pulled into our driveway, we saw that Mama had turned on the exterior Christmas lights before she left. The house looked festive, and Miller and I complimented her.

"Yes, sir, our best Christmas Forage yet," Mama said, looking at Miller.

The house was still dark when we entered, and the smell of garlic was mouthwatering.

"Your dad must still be out," Mama said. "Well, let's go ahead. It's too late to wait. Take off your coats and we'll eat our dinner."

I was starved and my stomach growled for the savory pork. We pulled off our heavy coats and boots, and together we set the dark wood dining table that had been in the McClellan family for generations. It still gleamed, and the scratches and nicks in the wood "gave the table personality," Mama always said. In short order Mama had warmed a crusty loaf of bread and set it on the table beside a dish of butter and some hard cheeses. She served the sliced roast and gravy on heaps of egg noodles with a green salad on the side. We feasted happily on our late dinner, talking about the play. Thor sat quietly at my feet and only once lifted his head to look woefully at me and then let his gaze shift to my plate in an obvious beg for some meat.

After we finished dinner, Miller brought out the ornaments we'd purchased at the Arts Council. We watched as Mama opened each one, taking great care. She oohed when seeing them: a delicate wooden carving of a shrimp boat, an acorn made from the paper of road maps, two red felt birds decorated with sequins, and a blown-glass dolphin.

Mama held each one up to let it hang from her

finger as she admired it. Each was pronounced "lovely" and "perfect."

Miller looked over to the corner of the living room where a few cartons labeled CHRISTMAS ORNAMENTS and XMAS LIGHTS were stacked against the wall.

"When do you think we'll get our tree?" Miller asked.

"Pretty soon." Mama reached for her coffee cup.

"Tomorrow's Christmas Eve!"

She took a sip and set it back on the saucer. "We're waiting on Daddy to finish that house job," she explained in a tone as if she'd given that explanation many times before. "He's been working so hard. Why, you know how he loves going out to cut the tree. It's tradition."

"All the good ones will be gone," Miller muttered with impatience.

"Does it matter?" I asked "Once we get the ornaments and lights on, it'll be beautiful."

This appeared to appease Miller because his face softened and he nodded with a half smile. "Yeah, I reckon."

Mama glanced at the clock and frowned. "It's awfully late. I wonder what's keeping your father."

"He must be earning a lot of money," Miller said, clearly relishing the prospect.

Mama smiled wistfully. "I hope so. Well"—she stood—"these dishes aren't going to do themselves. How about we get started? The sooner we get done, the sooner we can go to bed."

"I'd better walk Thor once more," I said, lifting my plate.

"I'll walk him," Miller volunteered. "It's my turn."

"Yeah, sure," I teased. "I know you're just trying to get out of KP duty."

We all laughed at that. Miller bolted out of the room to grab his coat and gloves and returned with Thor's leash.

"Come on, boy," he said after he hooked up the leash. "Let's go."

I watched as Thor trotted happily beside Miller. It was comical but I didn't dare laugh. Thor's head was almost as high as Miller's.

"Mutt and Jeff," I said.

Mama, catching the reference, laughed and shook her head as she carried plates to the kitchen.

Mama and I made short work of clearing the table and washing the dishes. We didn't talk much; we were both tired and eager for bed. We were just finishing when we heard the front door swing open. We hurried into the front of the house and saw my father standing at the door, wide legged, arms out. Or rather, teetering. The door was wide-open and the cold wind was blowing in. He weaved from side to side, his coat open and his cheeks ruddy, as much from drink as the cold.

"Oh." Mama's voice rang with disappointment as she hurried to his side.

"What?" he said in a belligerent tone.

Mama pushed him out of the way so she could close the front door. "You're drunk," she said accusingly.

"I'm not drunk!"

"I thought you were working."

"I was! Then me and Bill, we went out for a few drinks. It's Christmas, right?"

"Yes! It is Christmas! And you should have been with us at Miller's play. It would have been nice to have you with your family. But instead you got drunk!"

"I'm not drunk," he slurred back with less arrogance, weaving with the effort.

"You are drunk. And to think we were worried about you."

"No need to be. I deserve to enjoy the holidays a little, too." He staggered farther into the front room.

Something in the way he said that, angrier than anything else, convinced me trouble was afoot.

"Sit down, Alistair. I'll get you something to eat." Mama took hold of his arm to guide him to the table.

My father lifted his arm from her grasp and turned away, giving her his shoulder. "I'm not hungry."

Mama slammed her hands on her hips. "Did you eat?"

"I don't remember."

"Oh, great." She rolled her eyes. "Sit down, hear? I'll get you some water, too."

"I don't want any damn water. I need a drink."

"You've had enough to drink."

He shook his head and lifted his arms to ward her off. "I haven't had near enough," he said.

I moved forward to help my mother, but she waved me away firmly.

"No more drinking," Mama said, going toe to toe with my father. "Now stop it, hear?" She was mad now. "We were having a perfectly lovely evening, and you had to come in here and ruin it. Getting drunk . . . You should be ashamed of yourself. It's Christmas!"

I watched as his face mottled and he worked his jaw as if he were going to really fire off some choice words. My hands formed fists at my sides, ready to intervene. I could feel my heart rate zooming.

"Christmas, huh?" my father said angrily. "Let me tell you about Christmas." He said *Christmas* like a sneer. "I killed myself to make this deadline. You know I did. And I made it, too. Only a few piddly-shit things left on the final checklist to finish." He waved his hand so hard he teetered. "Not important. But is she satisfied? Nooooo." He drawled out the word. "She says she won't pay until the job is done. When I say I'll come back tomorrow to finish up, she gets all uppity and says it's Christmas Eve and she doesn't want any more work done until after the holidays. How it wasn't her fault the job wasn't done on time. The hell it wasn't!" he bellowed. "She changed her mind on the tile three times! Do you know how long it takes to get tile in?" He shook his head, then put his hand on his forehead.

He weaved a bit with his eyes closed and I thought he might stumble. Then he lowered his voice and said almost in a cry, "She's not going to pay me until after the holidays." He looked at Mama with his eyes red from drink and, though I shuddered to think it, crying. "I don't have the money I was counting on for Christmas. She stiffed me."

I felt for my old man. He had always been the rock that his family counted on. The Captain. He was the best out there and never disappointed. This final insult had to come as a crushing blow. My father had his disillusionments, too. I knew how much he'd sacrificed year after year, spending long hours on the sea doing back-breaking labor, to see it all go up in smoke. *Sometimes,* I thought grimly, *hard work doesn't pay off.*

Mama put her hand on his sleeve and was about to say something when the front door swung open again. Miller and Thor walked in. Miller was pink-cheeked from the cold night. With the dog at his side he never looked more like the innocent child.

"Daddy, you're home!" he exclaimed happily.

Daddy merely cast him a hooded glance, nodded brusquely, and ran his hand through his hair.

Miller unhooked Thor's leash. The dog trotted to my side, giving my father wide berth.

"I see that mutt is still here."

I frowned and put my hand on Thor's head in a protective gesture.

Miller sensed the tension, and I knew he'd do what he always did when Mama and Dad were fighting. He'd try to make peace.

"Hey, Daddy," he said in a cheerful voice, full of enthusiasm. He slipped off his hat and looked at our father, his eyes shining. "When are we going to get the tree? Tomorrow, right?"

It was a defining moment, and we held a collective breath. The voice of Christmas Present sang out in Miller's voice, full of possibility. *The Christmas tree!* It felt as though our entire Christmas was held in the balance. Mama, too, sensed the importance of this moment. She looked to Alistair, a silent plea in her eyes.

My father looked at my brother for a minute, processing Miller's words in his drink-sodden brain. Then his face wrinkled in scorn and the die was cast.

"We can't afford no damn Christmas tree!" he shouted. He slammed his arm down like a guillotine.

I saw my little brother's face fall, crushed in bewilderment.

"I'll buy the tree," I shouted at my father.

My father swung his head to look at me. I don't think he knew I'd been in the room until that moment. I saw shame flicker in his eyes, replaced too soon by a red-blooded fury fueled by alcohol. "No one gets a tree for my house except *me,*" he shouted, taking two steps toward me in a threatening move.

I bowed up, springing to defense mode. I felt Thor licking my hand, whining softly. Looking down, I could see him watching me with a worried look. He wouldn't take his eyes off me. I loosened my fist and began stroking his head nonstop.

"This is *my* house," Daddy shouted. "What I say goes. Got it? And *I* say we're not getting any damn tree!" He tottered on his feet, then swung his arm out in emphasis. "Christmas is a sham anyway. No one really gives a damn about anyone!" He scanned the room, going from face to face, his eyes glowering. He reared up and said with belligerence, "You can all forget Christmas." His eyes bulged as he dared us to argue. "We can't afford Christmas!"

"You're worse than Scrooge!" Miller shouted back at him, his hands in fists and his eyes glaring. "I hate you!" He turned on his heel and ran up the stairs.

Daddy ran after him, bumping my shoulder hard as he passed.

I felt a knee-jerk reaction, fight or flight, and I was gearing up for a fight. My head began to throb and buzz. I closed my eyes. I heard my father shouting . . . I heard men shouting . . . crying out. "The Carol of the Bells" was playing, mocking me as the pace went faster and faster. Anxiety . . . anger . . . danger . . . threat. I staggered forward.

Thor moved his big black body to block my path.

I felt my mother's hand on my arm. She caught my eye and shook her head firmly. "Stay out of it," she said in a low voice.

I blinked several times, focusing on her and where I was. I nodded yes, then took a deep breath. I looked down at Thor. He was watching me, assessing my anxiety. It was flight, I decided, and I grabbed Thor's leash. I retreated, following my brother up the stairs. Once again, the sound of doors slamming reverberated in our home.

Inside my room I felt the comfort of the cloaking darkness. With explosions going on in my head, light pierced like glass through my eyes. I slumped back against the door and took several more long breaths, letting my hand stroke Thor, finding comfort there, as I tried to stall the pressure building up in my head. In time I opened my eyes a slit and saw in the dim shadows the shapes of the Christmas packages I'd set on the floor by my desk. Among them I recognized the large rectangular shape of the painting I'd purchased for my father. I released a short laugh, thinking how many Christmas trees I could have bought for the price of that one small painting.

My skull felt as if it were splitting in two. I'd done too much. Tried too hard. I lay down on the carpet and covered my eyes with my arm. Thor came to lie beside me. I felt the power of his muscular body and the rhythm of his breathing. It soothed me, and as I wrapped my arm around him, I couldn't help but think of Miller and the night he slept here and also found comfort in Thor's presence.

We lay on the floor as I tried to gauge the power of this onslaught of pain as any surfer would an oncoming wave. This was a big one, I realized. It could last for two days. Right through Christmas.

I somehow managed to remove my shoes and belt and then crawl to the bed. As I lay in the darkness, I knew that somewhere in the room Thor watched and waited, listening for my cues. Knowing that, the knots of tension slowly released. Hours passed like this, and in time the pain lessened enough that I could process thought. I remembered my father's shameful drunkenness. I knew in the morning he'd be ashamed of his anger, his pettiness, but he'd never be able to take his words back. What he said came back to me now: "Christmas is a sham. No one cares about anyone."

For all my bitterness, I knew that wasn't true. I recalled my experiences in the shops. How many people had said, "Thank you for your service." I saw again the light in Miller's eyes when he said, "I think Mama will like this!" I felt again my pleasure buying my father that painting. And even more, the delight of stepping into the house and inhaling the scents of rosemary and garlic, feeling it was a home. And Mama's joy at receiving the simple ornaments.

Christmas was not a sham. My spiraling emotions were not triggered by anything that was done to me. Quite the opposite. I hurt because my brother hurt. I felt Miller's disillusionment. His disappointment. The loss of his innocence. I ached because I couldn't protect him from growing up.

Father is so much kinder than he used to be, that home's like heaven! . . . I was not afraid to ask him once more if you might come home; and he said "Yes, you should."

—Fan, Scrooge's sister,
A Christmas Carol

Chapter 19
Miller

I opened my eyes and knew immediately today was different. It was Christmas Eve. A day I looked forward to almost more than Christmas. I think it's because I liked the anticipation of Christmas as much as the day itself. I lay tangled up in my blanket. Usually I jumped out of bed and ran to the kitchen to see what treats my mama was cooking up. She liked to start her baking early. There would be cinnamon buns, my favorite. And scones, her favorite. She'd make bacon, too. I sniffed the air. I didn't smell anything at all coming from the kitchen, even though the sun was coming in through the window. That was odd. Then I had a terrible thought. What if she was doing what Daddy said and there would be no Christmas?

I felt a wave of cold wash over me. One that felt like fear. Could there really be no Christmas?

I already knew it wasn't going to be a great Christmas. I knew that the day I found out I wasn't getting my dog. But in the past few days things had started looking up. Taylor was beginning to be a bit more like his old self. Mama was cheering up, too. And then there was Thor. He was making everyone feel a bit happier. It was like he was some sort of Christmas angel.

Then Daddy had to go and ruin everything. He was worse than Scrooge. He was mean! I wished he would've just stayed away all Christmas. We were better off when he wasn't here. It made me mad to remember what he'd said last night. Telling us there was not going to be a tree. And no Christmas! Who said he was the boss of Christmas?

I could feel my blood boil just thinking about it. By saying we weren't going to have Christmas, Daddy made today feel worse than any ordinary day. It was like something was missing or taken away. Something important.

My heart felt heavy and I rubbed my eyes. They were dry and crusty from all the crying I'd done the night before. But it made me feel calmer. And hungry. Very hungry, especially thinking about all the food I didn't smell baking downstairs.

After a long while of listless lying in bed feeling sorry for myself, I was bored. I couldn't figure out how Taylor could stay in his room for so many hours. I pushed back my blanket, deciding I might as well get up. I rose and padded down the hall to the bathroom, noticing Taylor's bedroom door was still closed. That made me both sad and mad. He'd kept the door open the past few days so I could see Thor first thing when I woke up.

Downstairs, the kitchen was empty. My parents' bedroom door was closed. Wasn't anyone getting up today? I wondered. Was everyone just going to sleep through Christmas?

I went into the living room and saw the ornaments that Taylor and I had bought for my mother lying on the coffee table. The boxes filled with lights and ornaments for the tree were still in the corner, unopened. Mama had moved the easy chair out from the corner to make room for the Christmas tree. That was over a week ago. Every time I saw that empty space in the corner of the room, it made me feel bad. I mean, who didn't get a Christmas tree?

My lips tightened and I felt a surge of renewed anger. Daddy wasn't going to ruin Christmas, I thought. Not for me, not for Taylor, and, most of all, not for Mama. He didn't buy me my dog. I couldn't do anything about that. But I'd show him. He wasn't the only one who could get a tree!

I hurried upstairs, feeling like a man on a mission. I dressed warmly—long underwear, hiking socks, my thick boots—while my mind formulated my plan. I felt my blood racing. I was actually getting excited. I'd be the hero. I'd bring home the tree all by myself. I'd save Christmas for my family.

Maybe not all by myself, I thought again. I'd

never been foraging in the woods by myself. Mama had always come with me. Then it occurred to me that I'd be safe with Thor.

With that thought in mind I quietly walked down the hall and pried open Taylor's door, cringing when the hinges creaked softly. When I stuck my head in, Thor was already sitting up and watching me with those big dark eyes. Taylor was still sleeping on his belly, snoring.

"Thor," I called out in a loud whisper. I waved my hand. "Come."

Thankfully he came right away. I patted his head and guided him outside the room.

"Want to go for a walk?"

Thor understood that, and he pranced in joy down the hall, excited at the prospect of going out. The kitchen was cold, even at this late hour. Not even the smell of coffee. I moved quietly but quickly, pouring out kibble for Thor, adding extra to the bowl because I knew we'd be going for a long walk. While Thor noisily chowed down his kibble with relish, I made myself a bowl of cold cereal and wolfed it down, too. I kept an eye on the door and an ear cocked in case someone woke up and came into the kitchen. I wanted to sneak out before anyone could stop me. I put my bowl in the sink, then went to fetch my backpack from the hooks by the back door. I emptied the contents, a bunch of end-of-semester notices, onto the floor. Then I went to the pantry and filled it up with cookies, a box of peanuts, some raisins, and, with great luck, a stick of beef jerky. I tossed in a bottle of water, then, remembering Thor, added another. The backpack was getting heavy so I stopped there. We would only be gone a few hours.

That done, I donned my parka, hat, and gloves. Knowing I'd be in the woods, I wrapped a scarf around my neck. I was already hot and eager to get outside. Thor was watching me with happiness in his eyes, knowing we were going out. I often took him out for his morning walk, so he was used to me putting his leash on. I grabbed my back-pack, opened the back door, and we slipped out.

The sky was a grayish blue and filled with fat white clouds. The air tasted sweet and moist, a bit like rain. I didn't think it would and picked up the pace. Thor and I had made good time, dragging behind us the red wagon filled with my backpack and my father's ax. It was heavy but I could swing it. I was strong enough. I'd be able to cut down a tree, I felt sure. We were already at Mama's path—our secret path—into the great Marion National Forest.

"Come on, Thor. Let's find ourselves a tree."

Excitement thrummed in my veins as we made our way through the forest, following the well-worn path my mother and I had marched upon only weeks earlier. It seemed much longer ago since we'd gone for our Christmas Forage. On that trip Christmas had loomed as bright and rosy as all the holly berries we'd collected. Mama had said it was going to be our best Christmas ever, and I'd believed her because that was back when I still held hope I'd get Sandy. Back before Taylor had returned home with that awful PTSD. Back before Daddy ruined Christmas. I spotted several holly trees laden with rosy berries that my mama would surely have stopped for. I didn't want to go near their prickly leaves. It had been unseasonably warm that day, not cold like today. But I was warm in my heavy parka and dragging the wagon alone was hard work. The ground was covered with rusty longleaf-pine needles and a thick covering of damp, molding leaves. I was stupid not to think that Mama had dragged the wagon most of the way. My arm was getting sore and I worried a bit how I'd manage once the tree was in the wagon. But it was too late to chicken out now. Thor and I were on a mission, I thought, putting one foot in front of my other while dragging the rusty wagon behind me over the ruts and roots.

"We're going to find the most beautiful tree in the world," I said to Thor, bolstering my own resolve. He looked at me quizzically, wondering what I was asking of him. I laughed and reached out to pat his head. “Never mind. We’re almost there.”

At least I hoped we were. We’d been walking for what must’ve been hours. I couldn’t be sure because I didn’t have a watch. The deeper into the woods we went, the thicker the overhang of branches and needles and the darker it grew. I could hear birds calling from high up in the trees, and once I heard the high-pitched *kreeee* of a hawk and, looking up, saw one soaring over the tops of the trees. Daddy had told me that even from way up there, the hawk could spot a mouse running along the forest floor. As we hiked, I’d sometimes hear the sharp crack of a branch caused by something bigger than a bird. Much bigger. A deer, maybe? A coyote? I was glad I had Thor by my side.

“I reckon I won’t try to find the grove of trees Mama was telling me about. We’ve been out here too long already, and I don’t know about you, but I’m feeling a mite cold.” I looked up beyond the long stretch of towering pines to the bit of sky showing above. It was ominously gray, miserly with the sun. “We should head back. Keep your eyes open for any tree that would do for a Christmas tree.”

Thor looked at me and I swear he looked a bit anxious, like he was waiting for me to take him home. He stretched back, his long legs sticking out like logs before him. When he came back up, he gave a soft woof, as though telling me it was time to get going.

I was disappointed that I'd not found the famous grove of trees where Mama said the picking was ripe. But I wasn't discouraged. The Marion National Forest had lots of trees, and my tree was just sitting there waiting for me.

I just had to find it.

I continued down the forest path for what seemed like miles dragging that wobbly, rusty wagon behind me; then I saw the tree. It wasn't a great tree, I knew that at first glance. Its branches were spindly and few. But little acorns were on some of the branches and it was taller than me by half. It stood straight in an open bit of earth. Suddenly a shaft of sunlight broke through the clouds and shone smack on the tree, as if God Himself was pointing it out to me.

"That's good enough for me," I told Thor, and reached for my father's ax. It took more whacks than I thought it'd take to fell that puny tree. I was sweating by the time I'd dragged it onto the wagon. I put my hands on my hips, breathing heavily, and inspected the situation. The top half of the tree fell out of the wagon and dragged on the ground. I scratched my head, worried now. How was I going to get it home? I wondered. I hadn't planned on how to keep the darn tree in the wagon as I pulled. I should've brought a bit of rope. There was nothing for it but to choose—the tree or the wagon. I couldn't pull both.

"I can come back for the wagon," I told Thor. "But we need to get the tree home today. Tomorrow's Christmas!"

I dragged the trunk of the tree off the wagon and let it fall to the earth. Then I grabbed my backpack and slipped it over my shoulders. I wanted to eat more of those nuts, but I didn't want to waste any more time. Taking a deep breath, I bent to grab hold of the base of the tree. Suddenly Thor gave a loud bark and, like a bolt of lightning, took off into the woods.

"Thor!" I called out, dropping the tree. "Thor, come!" He didn't return. I could no longer see him, but I heard his barking fainter, farther in the woods. He'd probably cornered a squirrel or a raccoon, I thought as I took off after him into the deep woods. *Please, God, don't let it be a bear.* No matter what it was, I couldn't lose my brother's dog!

I am sorry for him; I couldn't be angry with him if I tried. Who suffers by his ill whims? Himself always.

—Fred, Scrooge's nephew,
A Christmas Carol

Chapter 20
Jenny

I couldn't remember when I'd last slept so late. I was up most of the night staring out the window while Alistair slept it off. I only went to bed in the early hours of the morning.

Alistair had been a handful; he usually was whenever he got drunk. Which wasn't too often, thank heavens, but when he did tie one on, it was a doozy. I finally got him soaking in a hot tub while I supplied him with aspirin and glass after glass of water. I would have been furious except that he'd wept. He felt so desolate, so worthless, coming up short at Christmas. I watched as he sat slump-shouldered in the steaming tub as all his sorrow, frustrations, and disappointment drained out into the water. When he was spent, I'd helped him from the tub, dried his wet skin, buttoned his pajamas, and brought him into our bed.

I couldn't sleep. I sat on the edge of my bed in a kind of stupor, wondering how everything had gone so wrong. I was sad for my husband. He'd been treated shabbily by the woman who'd hired him. No doubt the woman was using the checklist as an excuse to stingily hold on to her dollars until after Christmas. It was unforgivable. Coldhearted. Cap didn't deserve that treatment. No one could have worked harder, and with more pride in his work, than Alistair McClellan. Ask anyone.

I thought about all this and more in those angst-filled wee hours of the morning when all seems bleak. Only the bad thoughts, the worries and regrets, emerge in the middle of the night, like snakes when the sewers back up. I grew cold and my eyelids drooped heavily. I sighed wearily and lay down in my bed. I only knew that if I didn't get sleep, I'd face the new day less able—tired and cranky.

It was late when I fell asleep, and late when I awoke. The sun poured in from the open curtains and I had to use a hand as a shade while I opened my eyes.

"You're awake."

I turned my head toward the gravelly voice to see Alistair lying beside me. He was on his back and turned his head on his pillow to watch me. It was the same face I'd known for so many years, but his eyes were red, his stubble was dark along his jaw.

I felt a surge of disappointment. "I'm surprised *you* are," I told him tersely.

"I'd be dead if it weren't for your tender ministrations." He looked away. "The way I behaved last night, I didn't deserve them."

I wasn't sure that he did but kept my tongue.

"I'm sorry for getting drunk. I know that's no answer. I was just so angry." He emphasized the word *angry,* indicating to me the wound was still fresh. "I needed to douse the flames."

"What she did to you was wrong. She'll get hers; her kind always do. But it's only money. She's a cheater, a skinflint, a conniving . . . well, you know. But we'll leave it there. Don't bring that woman in my home. Don't give her the power to ruin our Christmas. Because she can't do that. Only you can."

Alistair lay quietly for a moment, and I wondered if he'd respond. I sighed and looked up at the ceiling, my arms straight at my sides. We lay beside each other but not touching. The distance between us felt vast.

In time, he spoke. "Say you'll forgive me."

"You didn't ask for my forgiveness."

He laughed shortly. "Wife . . ." He rose up on his arms to stare down into my eyes. "Will you forgive me? For without your forgiveness, the holidays mean nothing. Your love is all I need."

"Husband"—I slipped my arms around his neck—"I love you. And, yes, you're forgiven."

He bent to kiss me, but I laughed and turned my head and pushed him away. "But I won't kiss you smelling like a distillery. You stink, my love, and there's no easy way to say it."

Alistair fell back on his pillow with a groan.

"I feel like death warmed over." He pointed at me. "And don't tell me I deserve it."

"I won't. But I'll be thinking it."

He groaned again, softer this time, and put his arm over his eyes. I rose and went to the window to draw the curtains. The room slipped into a comforting gray light.

"Better?"

Another groan came as the response.

I went to his side of the bed and sat down closer to him. His eyes were closed but he wasn't yet asleep.

"Alistair, you'll have to apologize to the boys."

"I will." His voice was gravelly.

"And you'll have to go out with Miller and get a tree. I don't care if you cut one down, but don't come home without a tree. And a nice-looking one, too, for all the trouble you've caused."

Alistair pried open one eye. "Anything else?"

"Yes." I leaned closer to him. I waited until he opened his other eye and I had his full attention. "Talk to Taylor." I felt Alistair stiffen beside me. I reached out to lay my hand on his chest. "Don't shut him out with your cold silences and dis-dain. You shame him. He's still your son. Someone to be proud of. Help him, don't hinder him. Love him. Be his father. He's never needed you more."

"You're right. I'm not mad at him. Or ashamed.

I just don't know how to deal with his pain, and I'm afraid of losing him all over again."

"You can learn."

Alistair patted my hand on his chest. "You're right. I'll do better. I have to."

"You'll talk with him? Tell him you love him?"

He nodded slightly against the pillow.

I bent to kiss him. "Now go back to sleep. You're no good to anyone in this state."

I rose and dressed quickly, donning my old jeans, a long-sleeved red knit top that was getting threadbare at the elbows, thick green socks with candy canes on them—my fashion nod to Christmas—and my slippers, then left the room, closing the bedroom door behind me. Morning light filled the hall. I felt a renewed sense of purpose. The anger and angst I'd felt the night before had faded like an unwelcome ghost. In the light of day and Alistair's apology, I felt compassion for his disappointment, and though getting drunk was never the answer to a problem, I could forgive him. I was too old to hold on to a grudge. Too wise to let indignation spoil my day. Especially not on Christmas Eve.

The kitchen was empty and gray when I entered. A chill was in the air, and looking out the window, I saw that the sun only peeked out from behind massive, billowy clouds. I wasn't going out today. It could rain for all I cared.

I flicked on the overhead lights and headed for

the coffeepot. First things first. I made a big pot of coffee, knowing we'd all need a few extra cups of caffeine today. After a few bracing sips, I went to the cupboards and began pulling out my mixing bowls, spoons, and ingredients for my traditional cinnamon buns and scones. *There may not be fancy presents this year, but by God there will be good food,* I thought with satisfaction. I'd spent a good portion of my extra money buying an especially choice cut of beef for my Christmas roast. I'd handpicked each big baking potato and would twice-bake them with lots of butter and cheese. I even bought two pretty persimmons to decorate my salad. I glanced over to the bouquet of brilliant white lilies arranged in my best crystal vase. That was an extravagant purchase for my table, but if not for Christmas, when? I smiled at the prospect of a glorious day baking in my own kitchen and not cleaning someone else's!

Bacon was grilling, cinnamon buns were in the oven, and the scent of freshly perked coffee was in the air when Taylor emerged. I was dismayed, even disappointed, to see him unshaved and undressed. Yes, it had been a bad night, but it was time to rally. He squinted at me as though he was still half-asleep.

"Merry Christmas!" I called out cheerily.

He grimaced and brought his hand up to rub his temple. "Have you seen Thor?"

"No. Maybe he's in Miller's room." I stilled

my hand in the dough and leaned to better scrutinize Taylor's face. "You don't look well. Are your headaches back?"

"They never really go away."

"Your father feels very bad about what he said last night."

"Yeah, well, that excuse is getting old. He's not the only one having a hard time."

"I know." I returned to my dough. "But he's sorry this morning. And I think he'll say so himself." I straightened. "Want some coffee?"

He shook his head, then grimaced as though even that slight movement brought him pain.

"Does your new medicine help?"

He walked to the cabinet to grab a glass and filled it with water. He popped two pills into his mouth and took a swallow of the water. "We'll see." He turned to face me, perplexed. "Thor's not in Miller's room. I checked."

I made a face. "Well, he's not down here. Miller probably took him for a walk. I suspect he's making himself scarce."

"Can you blame him?" Taylor guzzled down the glass. He wiped his mouth with his sleeve, a habit I wasn't happy to see he'd acquired.

"Go back to bed." I returned to my scones.

He looked miserable and just waved his hand at me as he walked out. "Okay, then. I'm going back up. Send Thor to my room when they get back."

"I will. I hope your headache gets better."

I looked out the back windows. The sky was growing ominously dark, but the clouds were fat and white, not storm clouds. Perhaps there wouldn't be rain after all. Still, I hoped Miller wouldn't get caught in bad weather.

The cinnamon buns were iced and cooling on racks and I'd just pulled my scones out from the oven when I slowed down enough to realize I still hadn't seen Miller. The bacon was sitting on the plate already cold, with the fat congealed. Where was everybody? I wondered. Usually I had to chase the boys out of the kitchen. I washed the flour off my hands, and drying them on a towel, I walked to my bedroom. The morning was gone, yet Alistair was still sleeping. I quietly left and closed the door behind me. This was the first day he'd had off in I couldn't remember how long. Plus he needed to sleep it off.

I walked upstairs to fetch Miller. I didn't want him sulking and playing Xbox games in his room all day long. I knew he was still angry but didn't want him to dwell. He could help me with some of my fun shopping errands.

"Miller!" I exclaimed as I opened his door. I stared at the messed bed, the cold television screen, stunned that he wasn't here. Feeling a shiver of foreboding, I went to Taylor's room and, without knocking, opened the door. The lights were off and the curtains drawn, but I could make out his sleeping form on the bed. I scanned the room. Thor wasn't there.

Now I knew a moment of fear. Wasn't Taylor looking for Thor earlier in the morning? That was hours ago. Something was off. I could feel it. I hurried downstairs, made a quick tour of the house. The rooms were ominously empty without Miller or Thor. Feeling tension mount, I went directly to the coatrack by the back door. Sure enough, Miller's coat was gone, and so were his boots. Thor's leash was also missing from the hook. Where could he have gone? I wondered. And with a huge dog? An idea came to mind. Pursing my lips, I went directly to the phone and dialed a number I knew well.

Dill answered the phone on the third ring. "Hello?"

"Hi, Dill, this is Mrs. McClellan. Is Miller there?"

"No, ma'am."

"Was he there earlier?"

"No, I haven't seen him all day."

"Okay. Listen, will you call me if he comes by? I'm looking for him. Thanks. Bye."

My hand rested on the phone as I tried to piece together all that I'd seen and done since I had awakened. I remembered it was late when I went to the kitchen, a little past nine o'clock. Now that I thought about it, I'd seen an empty bowl in the sink and a spoon. So Miller must've awakened and helped himself to breakfast. What time would that have been? I felt a flush of shame. I didn't know because I wasn't up, as I normally was. As I should have been.

I ran my hand through my hair, recalling Taylor's coming in—was it ten o'clock? He was looking for Thor, which meant Miller and the dog would've been out for at least an hour already. Likely more. I glanced at my watch. It was nearly twelve thirty. No dog walk lasted that long. My gaze wildly scanned the room as panic filled my chest. Where could Miller have gone?

I ran to my bedroom now and pushed open the door and turned on the overhead lights. Alistair stirred in the bed, placing his hand over his eyes.

"Alistair!" I called. I went to gruffly shake his shoulder.

"Huh?" he answered groggily.

"Alistair, wake up," I said sharply, straightening. "Wake up! Miller's gone."

His hand slipped from his face and he blinked hard, his gaze sharp as the words permeated the fog in his brain. "Gone?" His morning voice was gruff. "What do you mean, gone?"

"I mean gone! I haven't seen him yet this morning. I just assumed he was in his room. But when I went up just now to check his room, he wasn't there. And Thor's gone, too."

"Probably took him for a walk."

"That's what we all thought, but for four hours? I called Dill and he's not there, either. I don't know where he is." My voice rose with panic.

Alistair coughed, then sat up, grimacing with the effort. After a moment he said, "No need to panic. He's probably out with some friends."

"With Thor?" I asked doubtfully.

"Maybe a pickup game or something." Alistair spoke calmly, but he was already rising from bed. "When did you last see him?"

"I didn't. He was already gone when I went downstairs."

Alistair didn't reply. He turned to look at the alarm clock on the bedside table. He walked to the window and looked out, checking the temperature gauge he'd affixed to the window frame. "It's not too bad out there." He rubbed his stubbled jaw. "Near forty."

I felt some reassurance knowing that.

"But there's no sun. And I don't like the looks of those clouds." Alistair's fingers began undoing his pajama buttons as he walked to the bathroom. "Bring me a cup of coffee, will you? I'm getting dressed."

By one thirty in the afternoon we'd contacted everyone we knew, gone to the school, checked the ball field, and even gone to T. W. Graham's, but no one had seen Miller or Thor. Everywhere people were bustling, doing last-minute shopping, and Christmas music was playing. For the first time the merry music grated on my nerves. By two, Alistair felt there was nothing left but to notify the sheriff's office.

Sheriff Cable was a handsome, likable man, tall and pink-cheeked, whose kindly demeanor masked a razor-sharp mind. His blue eyes were always twinkling with a smile, but if you knew him well, you also knew those eyes could flash with warning. Cable was near seventy, but no one in the county was fool enough to run against him. He knew most all by name, their history and whereabouts. Whenever someone was sick or needed a helping hand, Sheriff Cable was the first one there. He arrived promptly at the McClellans' house, accepted my offer of a cup of coffee, and began asking routine questions.

"Do you have any idea where he might have gone?"

I shook my head. "We went to all his usual places. Called his friends. All I know is he went out with Thor before nine a.m. and he hasn't been seen since."

The sheriff made a few notations in his pad. "Notice anything missing? His bike, maybe?"

I was dumbfounded. "I hadn't thought of that!" Alistair and I led the way to the garage. The old wood-frame structure, full of sand and spiders, was big enough for one car, Alistair's fishing boat, and his tools. Miller's bike was still there.

"The wagon is gone." I pointed to the empty space beside the wall.

"And so is my ax." Alistair pointed to the empty hook on the peg wall.

I looked at Alistair and we both had the same thought.

"I know where he went!" Relief rang in my voice. "He went to get a Christmas tree."

Sheriff Cable seemed amused. "You mean to cut one down?"

I nodded. "Yes. It's a family tradition. We were meant to go today but . . ." I cast a hooded glance at Alistair, who stood with his arms crossed and a frown of worry.

"Where would he go?" Sheriff Cable asked. "I can't think of a tree farm nearby."

"I told him about a place in the forest where my parents used go when I was a child," I explained. "I bet he tried to find it."

"In the Marion National Forest?" the sheriff asked incredulously.

"Yes."

"Ma'am, there's thousands of acres of woods in there. Where would we begin to look?"

"I know the path he'd take. I can take you there."

Sheriff Cable straightened and closed his notepad. "Then let's go take a look."

"We should get Taylor." Alistair looked around. "Where is he? I mean, where the hell are my sons?"

"Take it easy," I admonished, embarrassed in front of the sheriff. "I know you have a headache, but so does Taylor. One of his bad ones. He can barely open his eyes. Let the medicine do its job. He's no good in this condition."

I could see the disappointment flare anew in Alistair's eyes, but he kept his mouth tight and nodded in agreement. "Let's go then," he told Sheriff Cable. "We're wasting daylight."

The sheriff gathered a police search group and Alistair rallied the Old Captains. In any emergency on the water the Old Captains, a group of retired shrimp boat captains, would organize a search party of other captains and crew. They in turn alerted their families. This efficient system could activate the whole community in a short time. Quickly a group of fifteen gathered at the point of entry to the forest, within walking distance from my home, that for years I'd always used. It might have been an old logging trail back in the day, or used today by the foresters, I didn't know. But it made for a wonderful pathway into the woods for my private foraging. On this mean and dank afternoon the temperature was beginning to fall. Not at all like the gloriously sunny afternoon when Miller and I had last walked this path together so filled with Christmas cheer. The circumstances were terribly different today, I thought with a shudder. No one had to remark on the urgency of the situation. Time was not on our side.

Soon the forest enveloped us. Our feet fell loudly on the dried leaves and twigs, crunching along the narrow path. We were encouraged by signs of the wagon's wheels in the muddy parts of the path. Clearly we were on the right track, and knowing that spurred us on.

"There's the wagon!" I shouted, spotting it in the distance. I ran to the small clearing where the red wagon sat abandoned. The rest of the party, all men, gathered near, some calling out Miller's name, others searching the ground for tracks.

"Is that your ax?" asked Sheriff Cable, pointing to the one in the wagon.

"That's it." Alistair briskly nodded. He bent to look at the felled tree beside the wagon. Lifting the trunk, he tapped the bottom where sap oozed. "It couldn't have been cut that long ago."

"It still could've been hours," replied Cable soberly.

Alistair let the trunk fall to the ground and straightened slowly. "I'll pay the fine for my son cutting the tree without a permit."

The sheriff looked off. "Cut tree? I see a fallen tree. I don't see a cut tree."

Hearing that, I vowed the sheriff would have my vote for as long as he ran for office.

“Looks like he went this way,” called out a deputy. He stood at the edge of the clearing, pointing farther into the woods.

The sheriff scratched his jaw. “Now tell me why he’d go off and leave the wagon and the tree?”

“An animal might’ve scared him,” offered Captain Morrison. “There’s all kind of wildlife in these woods.”

“If that were the case, wouldn’t he have grabbed the ax?” the sheriff asked.

“Couldn’t say,” Captain Morrison replied. “Like I said, he could’ve been scared.”

“Bill, could you come over here and bring your map? The rest of you, gather round.” The sheriff waved his big hand to call the others closer.

Bill Chambers was a forester called in to assist the search. Lean and deeply tanned, he quickly took a map from his inside pocket and spread it out on top of the wagon.

“Where’d you say we are, exactly?” the sheriff asked, drawing near to the wagon.

Bill bent over the map and studied it a few seconds, then pointed to a spot on the map. “Here.”

The sheriff bent and drew an *X* on the spot, then drew two circles around the *X*. “Now this inner circle is about three miles in diameter. This outer one is six miles. Fifty percent of lost hikers are found in this here inner circle." He straightened and addressed the men. "Take a look and copy the circles on your own maps. Then let's split up in teams and proceed outward to the three-mile points on the circle. Keep whistling and calling, make lots of noise so Miller can hear you. If you find him, call it in on the walkie-talkie we issued. Likely your phones won't get reception in here. You can also blow on those whistles we gave y'all—three times. I'll stay here and set off a flare gun. Hopefully with all this noise and commotion we're making, he'll find his way back to us. We'll all meet back here in one hour. Four on the dot. It'll start getting dark. I don't want to have to send a search party for anyone else today. By nightfall, if we have to, we'll turn it over to SAR. Okay?" Satisfied with the response, the sheriff turned to me. "Missus, you ought to return straight home."

"No. I want to be here looking for him."

"Now I know you do," Cable said in a conciliatory voice. "But you need to be home in case your son finds his way back. We could be looking for him while he's safe at home and watching the TV. That doesn't make sense, does it? Why, he might be home already."

I could see the sense in that. "You'll call as soon as you find him?"

"Of course." He looked at me, his brows raised over bright blue eyes. "That goes both ways, hear?"

I smiled, appreciating his optimism. I walked to Alistair and we hugged, sharing our fear, despair, and hope in that one embrace. Then, without another word, I turned and made my way back along the familiar path. As I walked, I thought how quickly life could change. How just yesterday we were all upset about such things as holiday trees, puppies, presents. This day brought into sharp focus how meaningless those things were and what really mattered in this short span of time we spend on earth.

Glancing up at the sky, I prayed with each step that when I returned home, I'd find Miller sitting at the kitchen table, as I often did, his face smiling up at me when he saw me, calling out hello.

I returned home to find my son at the kitchen table, but not Miller as I'd prayed.

Taylor sat hunched over a grilled-cheese sandwich. He looked up when I entered, and his face seemed more relaxed, not tight with pain. "Where is everyone?"

I don't know if it was because I'd reached home and didn't find Miller as I'd hoped, or if I felt I could let down in Taylor's presence, or if I simply could not hold my angst inside any longer, but I burst into tears.

Taylor leaped to his feet and put his arms around me. "What's the matter, Mama?" His voice was the most tender I'd heard it since he returned home.

"Miller is missing," I choked out.

I felt Taylor's arms stiffen. "What do you mean, he's missing?"

"He went out with Thor early this morning. We found the wagon and your father's ax missing and figured out he went to the Marion National Forest to cut down a tree."

"You're kidding." Taylor wasn't joking. He was as stunned as I had been. He pulled back to look at my face. "He's been missing since ten o'clock?"

"Earlier. He was gone when I woke up at nine."

Taylor released me and put his hands on his hips, his face sharp with concern.

I quickly brought him up to speed. "Alistair and I looked everywhere, then notified the sheriff's office. A group of us went out to the path Miller and I take for our Christmas Forage trips. Sure enough, we found the wagon and a cut tree along the path." I lifted my hands in desperation. "But he wasn't there!"

"Thor was with him?"

"Yes, thank God. I feel much better knowing he's not alone out there."

"So what are they doing now?"

"They've broken into teams and are searching for him. We all have maps."

"Show me."

I pulled out my map and handed it to him. He immediately opened it and spread it out on the table. He pointed to the *X* that I'd marked as instructed. "Is this where he was last seen?" he asked tersely.

"Yes."

"Where's the entrance?"

I pointed that out as well.

He marked it with a pen, then folded the map in quick movements. He had become another person. His eyes were alert, his stance erect. He was in command. I thought this was what he must've been like in war.

"Why didn't you wake me earlier?" he asked tersely.

"You had a migraine. I thought—"

"No matter." He lifted his hand to halt my excuse.

"Taylor, don't go. It's going to be dark soon. I don't want both my sons lost."

"Don't worry, Mama. This is what I'm trained to do." He bent to kiss my cheek. "I'll find him and bring him home. I promise."

"I wish," Scrooge muttered, putting his hand in his pocket, and looking about him, after drying his eyes with his cuff: "but it's too late now." "What is the matter?" asked the Spirit. "There was a boy singing a Christmas carol at my door last night. I should like to have given him something: that's all."

—*A Christmas Carol*

Chapter 21
Miller

I followed the sound of Thor's barking through the trees, several branches clutching my coat and scratching my face. I called for him over and over, "Thor!" Finally I heard the thunder of his paws in the composted woods as he ran back to me. His tongue was wagging low and he had a goofy look on his face like he'd just had the best time. I wanted to be mad at him, but I was just so relieved to see him I put my arms around his neck and hugged him.

"Where'd you go, boy?" I asked against his velvety fur. He was warm and panting hard after his run, and his heat was comforting against my chilled body. Even with my long underwear I was starting to feel cold, and my fingertips were biting inside my gloves.

"This is as good a place as any to take a break," I told him, letting loose my backpack. It fell to the ground with a soft thud. I pulled out a few of the carefully packed snacks from the bag. I brushed away mold and bugs from a fallen log and sat. It felt great to give my legs a break. I was more tired now than I'd ever been on any of the Christmas Forages with my mother. Part of it was the cold. My fingers smarted in the few minutes I took my hands out of my gloves to parcel out the snacks. I shared my cookies and nuts with Thor, and he ate them greedily. Then I drank water from the plastic bottle. Even though the air was cold, I was thirsty from all the walking. I poured some water into the plastic cup I'd packed for Thor and held it out. This, too, he gratefully slurped up. I watched as he drank, amazed at how long his pink tongue was. When he drank the last drop, I put the cup back into my backpack and zipped it up. In the back of my mind I wanted to be sure I had some for later . . . just in case.

"As nice as it is to sit," I said to Thor, "we'd best get moving." I looked around to gauge which way I'd come running after Thor. We were surrounded densely by trees of every kind, mostly pine. Everything looked pretty much the same. I didn't have a clue which way to go. I felt a shiver of fear and walked around in a circle, hunting for a broken twig or footprints or anything that looked familiar. I saw depressed earth that could have come from my heels. It was the best clue I had.

"Let's go that way," I said to Thor.

Thor followed me trustingly, walking at my heels. But his tail was dragging low. I was feeling the cold in my fingers and toes and stopped from time to time to stick my gloves under my arms. I was worried about Thor. He didn't have boots on his paws. We plowed on through the forest, past thickets of trees so thick I had to detour. When I reached a small, open arena where soft, jagged-leaved ferns blanketed the ground, thick and lush like a soft green blanket, I stopped. My heart began to pound in my chest. I'd never seen this spot before. My mouth went dry.

"I think I made a wrong turn somewhere," I said to Thor.

Thor sat on the ground, his big tongue lolling out of his mouth, foamy at the top. I could see he was getting as tired as I was. I felt my first panic. I couldn't deny it any longer. I was well and truly lost.

I was feeling plain scared now. Thor depended on me to get him out of here. I tried to calm down and think back to when I went hiking in the forest with my Boy Scout troop. My Scout master had told us what to do in case we ever got lost. And the first thing he said was not to panic! To remember that my best tool was my mind.

I puffed out some air, then talked aloud to Thor, hoping he'd find comfort in the sound of my voice. Plus, it helped me, too, like I wasn't all alone in these big woods.

"We've been doing this all wrong. We need to stay put. We're getting tired walking around and have to conserve our energy. First we need to find shelter."

Thor followed me, sniffing the ground as I searched for someplace I could keep warm. A few yards off I spied a huge oak tree that looked like it had been struck by lightning. It was fried. The whole top was blown off and lay on the forest floor. It must've happened a long time ago because the inside of the trunk was completely hollow. It looked like some kind of cave, perfect for hiding in. I approached the mouth of the trunk slowly, afraid some critter might be hiding in there. Bears, large cats, snakes, and other unfriendly animals lived in these woods, and they'd be looking for shelter, too. But to my luck, the trunk was empty, save for spiders. A pine branch with needles was perfect for sweeping it out, then I added more soft pine branches to make a floor. I looked for a few more large pine branches to close us in and keep the cold out.

When I was satisfied I'd made a decent shelter, I pulled the red scarf from around my neck and tied it to a skinny sprout tree near my fort like a flag. At least if someone was looking for me, they wouldn't walk past me. I wished I knew what time it was. But it had to be getting late. The temperature was dropping as the sky darkened. I could feel something happening in the clouds, but it felt too cold for rain. I sure hoped it didn't rain. My toes felt real cold, too. I tossed my backpack into the shelter, then crawled in. The wood was burned and moldy, and it smelled musty inside the trunk. But the pine needles were pretty comfortable. All in all, it wasn't too bad, I thought.

"Come on in, Thor!"

Thor wasn't sure he wanted to come in to the cramped, dark space. He stood stubbornly at the entrance, legs wide and his big eyes staring at me with doubt. But I sweet-talked him and eventually he squeezed in beside me. It was right cozy in the dark space, like a cave. There was just enough room for me and Thor if he put his head on my lap. I was pleased I'd created such a nice fort; my Scout master would have been proud of me. But my pride was short-lived when I considered what a dope I was to get lost in the first place. And worse, how I'd not bothered to write a note telling anyone where I was going. Who'd be looking for me? I wondered.

"At least we have each other, don't we?" I gave Thor a squeeze.

His body warmth was comforting and I patted his head, hoping he was reassured. I figured if we could sleep here tonight, we could start looking for a way home tomorrow. I reached out to place the extra pine branches in front of our fort, closing us in. Once done, there wasn't a breath of wind. In the dim confines of our fort I heard my stomach rumble and realized it had been a long time since my snack. I wished I'd packed a proper lunch. I pulled everything I had left in my backpack out and divvied up the food. As Thor and I ate the remaining nuts, I wondered what Mama was planning for Christmas Eve dinner. It was usually a picnic before the fireplace, under the Christmas tree—thick sausages, pickled shrimp, chunks of cheddar cheese, Mama's biscuits, maybe some hot soup. Wine for the grown-ups, soda for me. Mama called it her fun dinner before her feast on Christmas. I missed Mama so much. I almost wept I was so hungry.

Light was fading. I packed my trash in my backpack and leaned back against the rotting wood, so tired I didn't care if there was a spider. I thought about the Christmas tree I had cut down and had left behind.

"You shouldn't of run off like that." Thor had to face the truth. It was his fault we got lost. "Now who is going to bring home the Christmas tree?"

Thor whined and looked at me with uncomprehending eyes. I couldn't stay mad at him. He didn't ask me to run after him, after all.

"Well, maybe we'll find it tomorrow on our way home. Yeah, in the morning we'll see our tracks and probably pass right by that tree. Then we'll drag it home, same as we planned."

That thought gave me some comfort. I was feeling warmer in the cramped space of my fort. Thor was like a space heater and he snored when he slept, louder even than my daddy. I felt my lids lower and I yawned wide, feeling the fatigue of the day's walking. I laid my head against the dog's velvety fur. Now there was nothing left for us but to wait. And pray.

“Good Spirit,” he pursued, as down upon the ground he fell before it: “Your nature intercedes for me, and pities me. Assure me that I yet may change these shadows you have shown me, by an altered life!”

—Scrooge, *A Christmas Carol*

Chapter 22
Taylor

Any hint of blue had leached out of the sky by the time I entered the Marion National Forest. Not a hint of sunlight was behind the graying clouds. I followed my mother's now well-worn path at a brisk pace, picking up at least a dozen footprints. I slowed when I spied Sheriff Cable in the distance beside what looked like my brother's wagon. I figured this was their ground zero. I didn't need the sheriff giving me directions, so I detoured, stealthily going east to the three-mile perimeter. I used my compass to guide me while I kept my eyes peeled for any sign of broken twigs, dog or human prints, anything. My guess was that if Miller had run off from his wagon and ax, he was chasing Thor. Thor could cover a lot of distance without taking a breath, so if Miller had run after him, plus walked for another couple hours, he more than likely was in the six-mile radius. That's where I headed first.

The woods swallowed me whole. In all directions the sights were the same to an unskilled eye. I was trained to see the minutiae, however. Bent branches, broken twigs. Pine needles when dry didn't bend when you stepped on them, they broke. At last I got my first break. I followed a narrow path where the moss was smashed, leaving prints much like on a thick carpet. I crouched low to the ground to read the signs. My heart beat faster when I found footprints in the pine needles and leaves. I rose and followed the trail for several more yards, then I spied a bit of black nylon caught on the end of a branch. I rubbed the fabric between my fingers. No doubt in my mind it came from Miller's parka. I lifted my head and sniffed the air in the faint hope I might catch the scent of smoke. I caught nothing but the crisp scent of pine and the pungent odor of molding leaves.

I wasn't disheartened. The darkening sky, the lowering temperatures, did not discourage me. I'd been through worse. I was a trained Marine. I had a mission. I felt stronger and sharper witted now that I had a purpose. I could use my skills again for the first time in months. I shifted the bag on my shoulders and kept going.

Another piece of good luck came farther up the trail. I found an empty plastic water bottle. I picked it up and put it in my pack. At least Miller had had the good sense to bring water, I thought. I figured Miller had been outdoors for at least seven hours. Most of the day the weather had been near forty degrees, a blessing. But on checking my temperature gauge, I saw the weather was nearing freezing as night was going to fall. Unbelievably, the weather reports predicted snow. I could imagine how many families were excited at the prospect of a white Christmas, so rare in these parts. For me, it was a complication. The snow would cover up any tracks. I looked up past the regal, tall longleaf pines to the small square of sky visible above.

A snowflake landed on my face.

Jenny

People were coming over to the house in droves, dropping off food. My table was groaning under the generous offerings. I looked around at the ten women who'd stayed with me to help ready the food for the search party, to tidy the house, and to keep me company. It was already half past four o'clock. I still hadn't received word from Sheriff Cable, but knew they'd be calling off the search soon. And not long after that the sun would set.

My boy must be getting real cold now, I thought with a shiver. *And frightened.*

I walked alone to the rear window of my kitchen, crossed my arms, and stared out into the shadows. Across my yard my neighbor's Christmas lights sparkled along her fence line like countless brilliant stars in the fog. Looking up, I couldn't make out any stars behind the thick cloud covering. Then I gasped.

"It's snowing!" I exclaimed.

The women in the room stopped what they were doing, and with high-pitched exclamations, they hurried to gather at the window and marvel at the rare sight of snow in McClellanville.

"The last time it snowed was the Christmas after Hurricane Hugo," Della said in her raspy voice. "December twenty-fifth, 1989." Della was eighty-six years old, as thin as a rail with a shock of white hair always worn in a bun. Della could still tell you the date and time of every significant event in the town of McClellanville.

"It's so pretty," remarked someone with awe, putting her hand on the glass.

"It'll make it hard to track," said Melissa Rogers, the town's manager. Someone quickly hushed her and looked meaningfully at me. Melissa was not one to be hushed. "Just saying," she said with a curt nod.

I didn't need to be told the snow wasn't helping the situation. I'd prayed all afternoon for the snow to hold off until after my boy was found. As I watched the gentle flakes fall soundlessly to the earth, I fought off despair. I couldn't give up hope, I told myself. I had to keep believing. Believe that Taylor would find Miller. I had to keep praying that my sons would return home.

Taylor

The snow was falling steadily now, big fat flakes, the kind children liked to catch on their tongues. I wondered if Miller was sticking his tongue out now, doing just that. This might be the first snow he'd ever seen, and the thought made me smile.

I shook my head. I couldn't get distracted. I took a deep breath and stretched. My muscles were tired; I was out of shape. But at least my migraine was gone. Looking down at the ground, I saw the snow was beginning to stick. That would cover the tracks. I was running out of time. I was losing the trail. I felt panic stir and had to fight it off.

"Dear God," I said, my words catching in the wind. I paused and bowed my head. I was too ashamed to pray. It had been too long a time. I had seen so much horror, witnessed the heartless cruelty of man to one another, and denied God's existence. What good were churches, I'd thought, if they inspired war? Instead I'd settled on the notion that all there was in this life was the here and now.

But here in the great woods I felt I was standing in God's cathedral. The beauty and power of his creation were both intimidating and inspiring. I was insignificant in the greater universe. Who was I to doubt if God cared about the smallest of insects hiding under the moss? Or these giant longleaf pines that towered like great pillars to the sky? I needed only to pray that He'd take pity on this one miserable, sinful, and lonely creature.

"Please," I said aloud, my voice piercing the deep hush of a forest snowfall, "I'm not asking for me. I'm asking for Miller. Help me to focus and be the Marine I once was. If You can do that, then I know I can find my brother."

Bringing up my head, I looked around to get my bearings and collect my thoughts. I knew enough about hypothermia to know that Miller wasn't near death. Unless he was wet, and there was no reason he should be, he had time. If he had his wits, he'd hunker down somewhere to keep warm. Miller was a smart kid. He knew the woods. Still, I was glad he had Thor with him.

According to my map, I was nearing the edge of the six-mile perimeter. But which direction had Miller moved in? I sensed I was close. That was the secret in the arsenal of the best trackers. Their intuition. I pulled out a whistle from my pack and blew it three times. The shrill sound echoed in the woods, sending birds fluttering and crying out. Again I blew. A moment later I cupped my hands around my mouth and called out, “Thor!” I counted to ten and shouted the dog’s name again. “Thor!”

I went still and listened. Around me the fat flakes swirled soundlessly in the crisp wintry air. I waited. Suddenly I heard a sound in the distance. I held my breath and lifted my cap past my ears. There it was again! A distinct bark.

“Thor!” I shouted again. “Thor!” I called, my heart pounding.

From the north I heard a great thundering, like a deer running. Turning, I saw a large black shape emerge from the woods. A dog . . . I lowered to my knees and opened my arms. Thor came running, eyes fixed, making a beeline for me.

“Thor!” I called again, and my dog was in my arms, whimpering with joy at finding me, licking my face, leaping like a puppy, behaving as though he’d not seen me in over a year. I didn’t know if I deserved such a welcome, but I felt the same at finding him.

I held his head in my palms, and Thor immediately calmed. We stared at each other, me and this stoic, loyal, brave-hearted dog. As I looked into his soulful eyes, I realized that this great animal had heard my call and come, not because he *had* to, but because he *wanted* to. He had faith in me. In my decisions. In my leadership. I saw shining in his eyes trust and more, respect.

In that moment, standing in the cathedral of

trees, we bonded. Man and dog, we were partners. I vowed that I would protect him, as I knew he would protect me.

"We're battle buddies," I told him, then pulled back and stood. "Now let's finish this. Thor, where's Miller? Find Miller," I commanded.

Thor was ready to act and made a curt woof. He walked a few feet to the north, sniffing the air, turned around, then came to stand again in front of me. His brown eyes were alert and intense. He woofed. He walked again down the path, then stopped to look at me as though to say, *Hurry up!*

"Good dog." I adjusted the pack on my back. I pointed. "Find Miller."

Thor took off with a lurch down the path. He knew where he was going. I paced fast to keep up with him as he thrashed his way through the woods. We hadn't gone far when he approached what looked to me like a burned-out hull of an ancient oak tree, so broad at the base a boy could hide in there. Then I saw the red scarf and I fist-pumped the air. Even in the dimming light the cherry red couldn't be missed. *Smart boy,* I thought to myself with pride.

I ran to the base of the great tree and pushed back the pine branches that covered the opening. Some of them had already been knocked down, no doubt by Thor when he leaped out. I leaned inside the cave-like space. It smelled of pine and mold, and though the light was dim, I saw Miller lying on a floor of pine needles. His eyes were closed, and for a moment I was afraid I was too late. I reached out to shake his shoulder gently.

"Miller," I said, loud enough to wake him.

To my eternal relief, his eyelids fluttered and then opened. His blue eyes met mine with a sleepy stupor, then widened with surprise. In a flash he leaped up and wrapped his arms around me, holding tight.

"I knew you'd find me," he exclaimed over and over, crying in relief. "I knew *you'd* be the one to find me."

I hugged him, not ashamed of my tears. When Miller pulled back, he was smiling, but I could see tears in his eyes, as well. And something more. Something far more compelling. I saw the pride that used to gleam in Miller's eyes when he looked at his big brother. I'd earned it.

And that, I knew, was the best Christmas present I could have hoped for.

I am as light as a feather, I am as happy as an angel, I am as merry as a school-boy. I am as giddy as a drunken man. A merry Christmas to every-body! A happy New Year to all the world!

—Scrooge, *A Christmas Carol*

Chapter 23
Taylor

The snow was collecting on the forest floor and along the tree branches, making the woods appear like a winter wonderland in the beam of my flashlight. We walked for some time in silence, listening to our footfalls crunching, with our breaths creating plumes of vapor in the cold air. I looked beside me often, checking on Miller. I worried that he was too tired. Frostbitten. We had no choice but to push on.

Suddenly I caught a whiff of something burning. I stopped and sniffed the air. I knew a moment's excitement and quickly reached into my pack to pull out my whistle. I blew it three times, the shrill sound piercing the quiet. Thor looked up at me, his ears twitching. Then I waited.

Not a minute later I heard an answering three blasts from a whistle.

"Over there!" I shouted to Miller, pointing.

We both felt propelled by adrenaline. Miller was tired, but his nap had given him the endurance to plow on. I blew my whistle again. Again we got a response. Picking up the pace, I followed the direction of the sound through the maze of trees, faith and my compass guiding me. Before too long we heard a mass of footsteps approaching, a chorus of sound after so much silence. Suddenly a group of men burst through the trees, headed by my father.

"Miller!" he shouted. He was wrapped in his heavy navy peacoat, a fur hat, thick gloves. His cheeks were ruddy, this time from the cold, and his blue eyes shone bright in the light of my flashlight.

"Daddy!" Miller called out, and ran forward into our father's arms.

Dad lowered to his knees in the snow and encircled my brother in his arms, his face buried in Miller's shoulder.

"My boy," he said in a choked voice.

No one missed the unspeakable joy and relief the Captain was feeling at finding his son. A few men stood watching with tears in their eyes. Others came to me to slap my back and congratulate me for finding the boy.

"Good job, Taylor."

"That's a Marine for you!"

"Where was he?"

"How'd you find him?"

I didn't notice their questions. I could not move. My father lifted his head and his gaze sought me out. When he found me, he looked straight into my eyes, held them, and nodded in gratitude. Then he rose and strode toward me with his hand out. I moved forward and took it, feeling the strength in it. But this time he pulled me against his chest and wrapped his free arm around me and firmly patted my back.

"Thank you," he said, his gruff voice shaking. "I'm proud of you, Son. Never forget that, no matter what. I love you."

"They're here!"

We walked into the house to an uproar of cheers. I stood near the entrance, stunned. It seemed to me most of the town was crowded into our house. It was déjà vu of my welcome-home party—was it less than a month ago? It felt so much longer in light of all that had happened.

"Miller!" Mama raced through the crowd directly to Miller and held him so long and so tight I thought he was going to pass out. But he held her just as tight.

"Don't you ever do that again!" she said without a trace of anger.

"Oh, Mama, I didn't know if I was ever going to get back home. But Taylor found me!" His eyes glistened. "I knew he would."

"Yes, baby, I knew he would, too!" She kissed him twice more, grinning wide. Then she rose and came to me, and this time her movements were slow. Her eyes were flooded with tears as she reached up to cup my face in her hands. She stood and looked into my eyes for the longest time. I basked in the pride and the love in my mother's gaze. All others around us seemed to disappear. At length, Mama said softly, "Thank you."

My chest swelled. To me, it felt as if she'd shouted it off the rooftop. "I promised you," I told her.

She hugged me and I caught scent of her perfume, the same she always wore. I would never smell that scent without thinking of my mother.

People were jostling us now, crowding in to slap my back, congratulate me. Smiling faces surrounded us, men, women, and children, tears in their eyes. Old Sheriff Cable was surrounded by people slapping his back and shaking his hand, telling him he was sheriff for life. He grinned and bore it with his usual good humor. The Old Captains beamed in the attention, fiercely proud of the role they'd played in the rescue. This was their town, after all. Forester Bill, the deputy, and other policemen were besieged with plates overflowing with food. A mug of beer was thrust in my hand. I raised it in a silent toast and drank thirstily. The joy in the room could not be contained. It was infectious. Each and every one came to hug the rescuers, then they began hugging each other, tears coursing down their faces, shouting out, "This was a Christmas miracle!"

"Merry Christmas!"

There was a fracas at the door and shouts of "Gangway!" My father, his face flushed and with snow on his cap, held the base of a tree in his arms. Some of his friends, also with snow on their caps and shoulders, held the tip as they plowed through the crowd across the room to the front corner by the window. They set the tree to a stand and I laughed out loud. It was the spindly tree that Miller had cut. Miller ran to the tree and stood spread-eagled, staring at it. His joy at seeing it could not be contained. And, too, his pride.

"I cut it down myself!" he announced to the cheers of all who heard. "It's the best Christmas tree ever!"

My father and his friends exchanged glances and chortled. No one would ever say a word against that puny tree.

More people were coming in and it was a bedlam of joy, greetings, and smiles. From a quieter corner where I stood with Thor at my side and a beer in my hand, I spotted Mrs. Davidson entering the house with Dill at her side. Her eyes were bright as she scanned the room. In her arms she was carrying a big, brown-eyed Labrador puppy.

"There he is!" Dill shouted, and shot forward through the crowd, calling out, "Miller! Miller!"

I grabbed Mama's arm and pointed her in the direction of Mrs. Davidson.

Her eyes widened and she looked around the room excitedly. "Oh my! Where's Miller?"

I took her arm and guided her to the corner where Daddy and Miller were standing. Mrs. Davidson was making a beeline for them as well. We all met at the tree.

"Miller, look who's here!" Mama exclaimed.

Miller already knew. His eyes were fixed on the puppy in stunned surprise. He looked as if he could've been knocked over by one of those soft, fat snowflakes.

Mrs. Davidson spoke to Cap. "I'd heard about what happened."

Alistair cleared his throat and leaned closer to Mrs. Davidson. He spoke quietly, but standing so close to her, I couldn't help but overhear.

"I'm, uh, sorry, but I wasn't paid for the job yet. I can't pay you till after Christmas."

"Oh, for heaven's sake." Mrs. Davidson grinned. "You don't think I'd let a little thing like that stand in the way of your Christmas gift! We're friends!"

I saw my father's mouth slip into a crooked grin of humble gratitude. "I'm obliged" was all he could get out.

Mrs. Davidson slipped the puppy into Alistair's arms. The puppy grunted and looked around the room with a bewildered expression. Thor came up to sniff the puppy's bottom, which made the puppy press away from the mighty nose.

Mrs. Davidson said, "I think you're the one who should hand over the puppy. It's your gift, after all."

Mama pressed Brenda Davidson's arm. "What's going on?" she asked sotto voce.

Mrs. Davidson's face was filled with emotion. "Cap wanted it to be a surprise. He made a down payment on this puppy weeks ago. But bless his heart, he made me promise not to tell anyone. It wasn't easy. I wanted to tell you that day Miller came to the house, but I just couldn't."

Mama put her fingers to her mouth and turned, eyes filling, to stare at Alistair. So did I. The jig was up. We all knew now why Daddy had been so devastated at not being paid before Christmas. The old Scrooge had planned a big surprise that would mean the world to all of us.

"Merry Christmas!" Mrs. Davidson said in a rush, and kissed Mama's cheek.

Alistair's smile was shaky and he seemed a bit shy as he turned to face Miller and held out the puppy. "Merry Christmas, Son."

Miller's face was pale with disbelief. Behind him, Dill was grinning ear to ear, no doubt relieved to be able to share the secret at long last. He nudged Miller forward. "Go on. Get him!"

Miller stumbled forward and reached out his arms. Alistair carefully shifted the puppy into them. Miller closed his eyes and laughed as the puppy began licking his eyes, his nose, his face, in excitement.

"Careful he doesn't pee on you," Dill said.

"I don't care if he does," Miller replied, laughing.

Mama walked swiftly to Alistair and put her arms around him. "Thank you. Thank you for the best Christmas."

Someone turned on Mama's CD player, and Bing Crosby sang out "White Christmas" through the room. The irony was lost on no one as everyone burst out laughing and toasted the snow. Now that Miller was safe at home, we could all relax and enjoy the rare sight of the flakes gracefully swirling in the night air outside our windows.

Everyone started to sing with the crescendo of the song. I led Thor through the room, grabbed my coat from the back of a chair, and, slipping it on, walked out the front door. The crisp, cool air felt fresh and welcome after the press of the crowd. I couldn't have endured it without Thor. My hand had never left the soft fur of Thor's neck throughout the emotional scenes. But it was all good, I thought to myself, breathing out a plume of air in relief.

The snow fell soundlessly around me. I appreciated the relative silence, broken only by the muffled sound of the party's singing. I pulled up the collar of my coat and walked with Thor trotting happily at my side, down the front walkway to the sidewalk.

"Which way?" I asked Thor.

He looked up at me, total trust in my decision shining in his eyes.

I grinned. "Right, then." I paused to look in the front windows of my home. I caught a glimpse of the spindly tree and, beside it, Daddy standing with his arm around Mama. Miller was still holding his puppy, and I laughed, imagining he wouldn't let go of that pup all night.

I looked around at the dark night. The street-lamps illuminated the white flakes as they twisted and twirled in the air, so fat they looked like feathers falling from the sky. "A white Christmas," I said aloud, hearing the disbelief in my voice. I stood and watched the flakes fall for several minutes, feeling the rarity of the moment. Even the magic. We all knew the snow wouldn't last. It might even melt at sunrise.

But for tonight, everyone agreed it was a miracle.

I will live in the Past, the Present, and the Future!

—Scrooge, *A Christmas Carol*

Epilogue

CHRISTMAS EVE 2015
SEA BREEZE, SULLIVAN'S ISLAND, SC

Taylor

The doorbell of Sea Breeze rang. Thor jumped up and barked his warning, then immediately trotted off to the front door. The baby startled at the noise and commenced crying. Harper cooed and brought the baby up to her shoulder.

"That'll be them," Mamaw announced, setting down her knitting. The pink and white yarn was taking the shape of a petite sweater for her namesake.

I smiled in anticipation of our guests, set down my drink, and walked to the front door of Sea Breeze. The historic house has been in Harper's family for generations. It was one of the early summer cottages on Sullivan's Island and a family treasure. Each nook and cranny was filled with charm, memories, and history. I'd met Harper in this house. Fell in love with her here. Married her and had our first child here. My best memories were now embedded in Sea Breeze.

This was my home now, too. Even after six

months of marriage I had to remind myself of this. I made my way through the gracious living room to the front door. Thor was already there, prancing in excitement. Swinging open the door I saw the faces of my family clustered on the front porch—Daddy, Mama, and Miller. Miller's dog, Sandy, stood by his side, straining at the leash, almost as large as Thor. I laughed when I saw the dog was wearing a Christmas-themed bow tie.

"Merry Christmas!" I called out, and opened wide the door, ushering them in. The front door wore a wreath of holly and the night air was relatively balmy. Thor and Sandy immediately pounced on each other, old friends, and greeted each other with a hearty bout of sniffing.

One by one my family passed me, each delivering the requisite hug and kiss. Each was bundled down with gifts. Mama entered in a beautiful red sweater twinkling with festive sequins. There were a few more silver strands in her hair but she was as beautiful as ever. She was carrying a large bouquet of flowers for Harper. When she leaned in close to kiss me I closed my eyes and inhaled her unique scent.

Daddy strode in behind her in his best tweed jacket. He was a bit broader in the beam these days, more gray in his hair, his big arms filled with gifts. "Hey, Son," he said in a booming voice, filled with joy. "Merry Christmas!" His eyes searched over my shoulder. “Where’s that baby?”

“Merry Christmas, Dad,” I said, slapping his back. “Go on in. Harper’s waiting.”

Miller came in last. At fifteen he’d changed the most. He was already as tall as me but hadn’t yet filled out. He was lean and lanky in his green sweater over a checked shirt and tan trousers. And he was a looker. His brown hair had Mama’s waves and his blue eyes shone under long lashes.

“I got you something,” Miller told me, and handed me a small package clumsily wrapped in red paper with lots of tape. “I wanted to give it to you without everyone being around.” He looked up to check that the family had gathered in the living room. “It’s not very good. I mean.” He laughed with embarrassment. “I made it myself. It’s from the tree we brought home that night years ago. You know, the night you saved me.” His face colored. “Well . . . you’ll see. Merry Christmas.”

I took the package and looked at him quizzically. “Should I open it now?”

“No,” he replied quickly, and shook his head. “Just when you’re alone.”

With that he grinned sheepishly and walked into the room, calling Sandy and Thor to his side with a few claps of his hands.

I paused at the door and watched my family

greet one another with heartfelt kisses and echoes of "Merry Christmas." Taking this quiet moment I slipped away down the hall and out of sight. I tore open the red paper of Miller's gift. Inside lay several wood discs sliced from the bottom of a small tree. On each disc was handpainted a white snowflake. He'd drilled a hole at the top of each for the red, white, and green ribbons. There were four of them, and on the back he'd written the names of my family: Taylor, Harper, Marietta, Thor.

I felt humbled by the thoughtfulness of my brother's gift. These discs were made from the spindly Christmas tree that he had cut down that fateful Christmas he'd gotten lost in the woods. What had he said? *"The night you saved me."*

Oh, Miller, I thought to myself as I looked down at the wood ornaments. *That was the night you saved me.*

I followed the sounds of cheerful conversation and clinking glasses to the foyer, then paused before entering the living room. I wanted to savor the moment. The fire crackled in the hearth, stockings hung over the mantel, carols played, and in the corner stood our robust Christmas tree. It was Harper's and my first Christmas tree together as husband and wife. Our baby, Marietta's, first as well. We didn't have many ornaments yet. Harper had hung several white sand dollars with red ribbon and there were several palmetto frond flowers, treasures that had been handmade by Lucille, a longtime friend of the family. It seemed as if the whole house was encased in fairy lights. I thought to myself, *This was a classic Christmas scene.* It could be a painting. Or the last scene in a movie. Maybe it was only because I saw the scene through the veil of sentiment. No matter. I would remember the scene forever.

With an urge to be part of it all, I strode into the room and walked directly to the tree. There I began to hang the four wooden ornaments on selected bare spots of the leafy branches. One by one the family gathered around the tree to look at them. One by one, they exclaimed how wonderful the ornaments were.

"What a clever idea!"

"Did you make them yourself, Miller?"

"I'll never forget that tree."

Caught in the moment we began exchanging ornaments. This was a new holiday tradition. Ever since that homecoming Christmas five years earlier we McClellans came together on Christmas Eve to exchange ornaments and decorate the tree that my father and Miller had cut down together. This was the first Christmas I could welcome my family to *my* home to decorate the Christmas tree I had felled.

The tree had become our unspoken symbol of that important Christmas when we had all dug deep and fought for one another—for our survival. For our family. For our happiness. And in the process, discovering the true meaning of Christmas.

Mother received four wooden ornaments from Miller just like the ones I'd received, only hers bore the names: Jenny, Alistair, Miller, and Sandy. Mama and Dad gave us a crystal picture frame that held a photo of Marietta and the words *Baby's First Christmas*. Mamaw presented us with a handblown glass dolphin.

I turned from the tree to watch my father settle on the sofa with the baby in his arms. He bent over her, cooing, utterly besotted. Harper hovered nearby, beaming.

"Look at her hands!" Daddy exclaimed, looking up. "A fisherman's hands, I tell you."

"Fisher*woman,* you mean," Mama corrected him. She beamed and said to Mamaw, "I finally got my girl!"

Mamaw agreed with a conspiratorial smile. "I'm so fortunate to have my three."

"Girl or boy, I'll have a fishing rod for her by the time she can walk," Daddy announced.

Mama turned to me and smiled a bit possessively as her gaze captured my face. "You look quite handsome." She patted my gray cashmere jacket over my red-checkered shirt.

"Harper gets all the credit," I replied. "Except for the tie." I lowered my chin to look at the green silk tie emblazoned with Christmas trees.

"You gave me the tie last Christmas. Don't you remember?"

Mama laughed. "I did, didn't I?" Then her gaze swept the room, a quiet smile of deep contentment on her face. "Oh, Taylor," she said with a sigh. "This was my Christmas wish for you five years ago. All this . . ." She turned her gaze to meet mine. "I'm so proud of you."

I looked at her for a long moment. We knew each other so well.

"No headaches?"

"No. All good."

"That, I suspect, is all Harper, too."

"Don't sell yourself short." I bent to kiss her cheek. Again, I caught her scent at her throat and it carried me back through a lifetime of Christmas memories. "Thanks, Mama. For always making Christmas special for us."

My words struck true and she appeared deeply moved. "That's a mother's job."

"Speaking of a mother's job." I looked over my shoulder. "You should rescue Marietta from Daddy. I think she's had enough fishing lessons for a three-month-old."

"I'm on my way," she whispered. Walking across the room, Mama said loudly, "It's my turn to hold the baby!"

With everyone engaged, I went to the tree where dozens of gaily decorated presents reached the bottom limbs to pull out a small package. Then I crossed the room to where Miller sat on the floor with Sandy and Thor on either side.

"Quid pro quo." I held out a small package wrapped in green with a white bow. "For you."

Miller looked up from the dogs to take the package. He hefted it up, checking its weight, then said with a teasing frown, "Feels like a book."

I laughed. "Open it."

Harper glided across the room in her long emerald green silk dress that made her red hair shine in contrast. She was carrying a tray filled with champagne flutes. The consummate hostess, she leaned in close to my ear, discreet.

"We aren't opening presents yet," she admonished quietly. "My sisters haven't arrived."

"I know. This is personal." I kissed her nose, then turned to watch Miller. I wanted to catch his reaction.

Miller opened the wrapping and found that it was, indeed, a book. He turned it in his hand to view the cover. Then his face eased into a knowing grin of pleasure.

"*A Christmas Carol*," he announced. "Excellent."

"No 'bah, humbug'?" I asked.

Miller shook his head. "Like you said. It's a classic." Then he slanted a gaze my way and added wryly, "And we'll always have Marley's Ghost."

I guffawed at our inside joke.

"Am I missing something?" Harper asked.

"It's a long story," I told her. "With a happy ending."

The doorbell rang again and this time two dogs leaped to their feet and ran for the door. Sandy was barking up a storm. Marietta startled once more but she quickly settled with my mother's rocking and cooing.

"Thor!" I called out. Immediately Thor came to my side and, chastened, sat quietly. Miller's dog, however, was raising a raucous. Miller hurried after his dog to stop the cacophony of barking.

"Your dog could use a few lessons," I teased him as he ran past.

"Where's Clarissa when we need her?" he called back.

Mamaw stood at the front window, a vision of pale blue silk and cashmere. A long strand of pearls draped her chest. She pushed back the drapes and looked out. "Why, it's the girls!" she exclaimed, clasping her hands together. "Oh, this is a party now!" she said to her companion, Girard, who stood by her side, looking elegant in his vintage smoking jacket. She took his hand and together they hurried to greet the family at the door.

The sound of high-pitched voices floated in from the front door, punctuated by heavy male laughter.

“I hope we’re not too late!”

“We had champagne at Dora and Devlin’s on the way. They’re right behind us.”

More voices rose up. More welcomes.

Mamaw’s voice rang out in her delicate drawl, “Come in! We’re waiting for you. The bubbly is all poured!”

Nate bolted into the room, heading straight for the presents under the Christmas tree.

The rest of the Muir family entered as a wave of glittering color and smiles—Blake and Carson, Dora and Devlin, Atticus and Vivian. Harper passed out flutes of champagne to all but Carson, who didn’t drink alcohol, and Dora, who, pregnant, settled for bubble water under Devlin’s watchful eye. Now that everyone in the family was here, Christmas had begun in earnest.

I went to the coffee table and picked up my dog-eared copy of *A Christmas Carol*. I’d purchased it five years earlier when helping Miller with his book report. I’d read *A Christmas Carol* many times over after that pivotal Christmas. The more times I read Dickens’s prose, the more I understood and took heart at his underlying message: We all had the chance to redeem ourselves, no matter how much of a Scrooge we may be.

I’d journeyed so far from that Christmas five years ago, when I’d returned home a broken man with PTSD. I’d learned to accept my past, embrace my present, and I held bright hope for the future. Most of all, I was not alone. I had Harper, Marietta, and Thor at my side. I'd been transformed. Dickens never wrote truer words when he had Scrooge exclaim, *"I shall live in the past, the present, and the future!"*

All were gathered in the living room, drinks in hand. I stepped forward and raised my glass. The family quieted, eyes on me filled with expectation. Then, with a wink in Miller's direction, I made a toast inspired by the book that had helped carry me from my dark days to the happy, grateful son, brother, husband, and father I was today.

"God bless us, every one!"

Recipes

The holidays are a time for families to gather together to share stories, gifts, laughter, and love. It's also a time to feast! Each culture has unique, traditional foods celebrated at the holidays. Likewise in the lowcountry—that very special geographic region along South Carolina's coast that I call home. Here we delight in a bounty of foods born from our local agriculture and marine life. Think shrimp, barbeque, sweet tea, pecans, rice, and you're just getting started.

The queen of Southern cooking is Nathalie Dupree. South Carolinian Nathalie Dupree is the celebrated, bestselling author with more than three hundred television appearances for the Food Network, PBS, and the Learning Channel. I am a lucky woman to also call Nathalie my friend. Of course I turned to her when I was searching for holiday recipes to include in *A Lowcountry Christmas*! Nathalie promptly responded with the recipes included here. All recipes can be found in the James Beard Award–winning cookbook that is a must-have for any Southern cook: *Mastering the Art of Southern Cooking.*

Nathalie prepared the Chocolate Snowball recipe for a private luncheon. It's been my

Christmas dinner dessert ever since. Every recipe is delicious and a perfect choice for your holiday table.

My favorite distillery is, of course, Firefly Distillery! They created the delicious signature cocktail for *A Lowcountry Wedding*. For *A Lowcountry Christmas*, Firefly again created a signature cocktail. Be sure to include it for your parties!

Cheers!

Mary Alice Monroe

Pickled Shrimp, or "Swimpee"

Makes 2 pounds

I couldn't resist using the name of this recipe from *Charleston Receipts.* It got this name from the vendors who early on walked the streets of Charleston calling out "swimpee" to sell their wares. The recipe, however, is my own. This recipe doubles easily.

2 pounds shrimp, cooked and peeled
3 large sweet onions, sliced
¾ cup olive oil
1 cup sherry vinegar
Salt
Freshly ground black pepper
Fresh herbs to taste, such as lemon thyme or lemon balm
Lemon slices, optional

Starting with the shrimp, layer shrimp and onions in a large glass bowl.

Mix oil and vinegar, and season to taste with salt and pepper and herbs. Pour this mixture over the shrimp and onions, and cover tightly. Refrigerate overnight or up to two days.

Herbed Shrimp and Scallop Ceviche

Serves 8

Cool shrimp and scallops are enticing in a glass bowl at a buffet. They can also be served with toothpicks for nibbles or on plates as a first course for a sit-down meal.

We know ceviche was served by Martha Washington in early colonial days (spelled *caveach*), most likely wending its way here from the Spaniards in Mexico and Latin America as well as from Barbados and other islands. This is easy, fast, and beckoning, and is best made a day or two ahead. Poaching the seafood very quickly before marinating takes away the trepidation some people have about eating "raw" seafood.

1½ pounds large raw shrimp in shells
½ pound raw sea scallops, sliced horizontally into ½-inch pieces
Grated rind of 3 limes, 2 lemons, and 1 orange, no white attached
⅓ cup fresh lime juice (about 3 limes)
¼ cup fresh lemon juice (about 2 lemons)
⅓ cup fresh orange juice (about 1 orange)

5 tablespoons fresh parsley, thyme, oregano, and basil, chopped
½ small red onion, very finely chopped
¼ cup olive oil
½ to 1 teaspoon hot sauce, optional
Salt
Freshly ground black pepper
1 teaspoon commercial seafood seasoning or Creole seasoning, optional
1 large avocado, peeled and sliced

Bring 2 quarts of water to a boil in a large pot. Add the shrimp and poach just a few minutes, until tender and pink. Remove the shrimp with a slotted spoon or strainer, reserving the poaching liquid, and set shrimp aside to cool.

Return the poaching liquid to a boil. Move the scallops to a heatproof strainer or colander and dip into the boiling water for about 30 seconds, until the scallops are just cooked. Remove and set aside to cool. Peel the cooled shrimp and cut into thirds. Move the scallops and shrimp to a plastic ziplock bag. Add the grated lime, lemon, orange rinds, and the juices. Refrigerate covered, and marinate overnight, tossing occasionally.

When ready to serve, bring to room temperature and drain, reserving the juice. Add the herbs, onion, oil, and hot sauce, and toss lightly. Season to taste with salt and pepper.

Taste and add optional seafood seasoning as

desired. Serve chilled with the avocado. It looks smashing in a stemmed wide champagne glass with a wedge of avocado.

Caveach, a noun for "pickled mackerel," is also a verb that refers to the "cooking of raw fish" using lime juice or other acid. Known in early American cookbooks as *ceviche*—also spelled *cebiche* and *seviche*—this acid "cooking" actually brings about a change of appearance and texture associated with cooked fish but, in fact, does not actually cook it. In French, Spanish, and Portuguese, *escabeche* is a similar term but refers to the pickling of cooked fish.

Spicy Sausage Balls

Makes 100 to 120 balls

This makes a gracious plenty, but the recipe can be cut down proportionally quite easily. Any extra sausage balls can be frozen cooked or uncooked. Chilling the dough makes it easier to work with. The self-rising flour gives it the punch that makes it special.

1 pound hot pork sausage
1 cup self-rising flour
1 pound grated sharp Cheddar cheese

Preheat oven to 400 degrees.

Mix together sausage, flour, and cheese with hands to form a dough, or move to a plastic ziplock bag to massage the ingredients together to form a well-incorporated dough, and refrigerate for 20 to 30 minutes.

Divide the dough into 4 pieces. Working with one piece at a time and keeping the remainder refrigerated, take 1 tablespoon of cold sausage mixture and using hands or a melon baller, roll it into a ¾-inch ball. Move to a rimmed baking sheet, leaving a small space between balls. Repeat with remaining dough.

Bake 15 minutes. Balls will puff slightly when cooked. Remove pan carefully from the oven, as there will be hot fat on the pan. Discard the fat and serve the sausage balls immediately. They can be refrigerated overnight and reheated, or wrapped well and frozen.

EVALUATING SAUSAGE SEASONING

Usually sausage has a sufficient amount of seasoning, but it's always a good idea to sauté or microwave a small amount of sausage to know how it tastes before proceeding to add other ingredients. It might need more salt, pepper, or spices, depending on your taste.

A Mess of Greens and "Pot likker"

Serves 6 to 8, including "pot likker"

A "mess" of greens, as cooked greens are called, is an armful of bundles of turnips or collards that cook down to a quart of greens in addition to the broth. Regarded as a comfort food, greens can be a meal, eaten just by themselves, or with cornbread or biscuits, as well as part of a larger meal.

When meat was a rarity, the seasoning meat in greens was an important dietary supplement, with the fat giving energy for long days and cold nights.

Greens are best when picked after the first frost, customarily around hog butchering time, when there is a snap in the air, or in early spring; but there is hardly a time anymore when they are not available.

⅓ pound sliced, rinsed salt pork or streak o' lean, smoked neck, or other cured pork
1 to 2 slices onion, optional
1 small hot pepper, optional
5 pounds turnip, collard, poke sallet, or kale greens, washed

Salt
Freshly ground pepper
Hot sauce, optional

Bring ½ gallon of water to a boil; add the pork, optional onion, and hot pepper and return to a boil. If time is available, cook half an hour or so to flavor the broth.

Meanwhile, tear and discard from the greens the stalks and any tough veins. Tear or cut the remaining greens into pieces and add to the broth.

Return to a boil, reduce the heat to a simmer, pushing any bobbing greens down into the liquid, and cover. Cook 50 minutes to 3 hours, as desired. Take a pair of large scissors and cut any pieces of greens larger than bite-size. Taste and season with salt, pepper, and hot sauce as desired. Serve with the broth (pot likker), or strain, reserving the broth for another time. Cooked greens will last covered and refrigerated for several days. They freeze up to 3 months.

OPTIONAL PREPARATION:

When the greens have returned to a boil, add peeled and cut-up turnips or beets, and cook until the vegetables are done, about half an hour, depending on size.

Add small pieces of potatoes to the boiling greens and cook until the potatoes are done, about 30 minutes, depending on size.

Break up pieces of cornbread and add to bowls of pot likker as desired.

Many Southern homes used to keep a bottle of vinegar infused with peppers on the kitchen table (the closer to Louisiana, the hotter the concoction). Greens were sprinkled with vinegar or hot sauce before eating.

Hoppin' John

Serves 6 to 8

A must-do dish at New Year's and other holidays, the peas represent good luck and health. Traditionally, since this was a New Year's dish, the peas were dried, but, of course, canned or frozen are readily substituted and seen nearly all year long.

- 2 cups dried black-eyed peas, lady peas, or cowpeas
- 1 piece fatback, hog jowl, or other smoked meat, slashed in several places
- 1 hot red pepper
- 1 medium onion, chopped
- Salt
- Freshly ground black pepper
- 1 cup uncooked rice
- 4 tablespoons drippings, preferably bacon

Pour boiling water over the dried peas to rinse in a large pot and set aside while preparing other ingredients. When ready to proceed, drain the peas and discard the water. Add fresh water to cover the peas. Add the fatback, hot red pepper, onion, salt, and black pepper. Bring to a boil;

cover, reduce heat, and simmer until the peas are nearly tender, about 45 minutes to 1 hour, skimming off the foam as needed. Add more water as needed to cover the peas. Continue cooking, covered, until the peas are tender. Remove the peas with a slotted spoon, reserving enough liquid in the pot (about 3 cups) to cook the rice.

Bring reserved liquid to a boil, add the rice, and return to a boil. Cover. Reduce heat and simmer until the rice is cooked, about 30 minutes. Return peas to the pot, stir together, and cook for a few minutes more. Add drippings to flavor the dish, taste, and adjust seasonings. Turn out into a large dish and serve. This may be made into a tasty salad at a later time.

Chocolate Snowball

Serves 6 to 8

Imagine a deep, dark ball of chocolate, iced with snowy white whipping cream. Now imagine it as big as a bowl, as easy to serve and cut as a cake, and even easier to make using a food processor or mixer. It doubles easily—making one gigantic ball or 2 dinner-party-sized ones.

1 (10-ounce) package semisweet chocolate chips
½ cup water
1 cup granulated sugar
1 cup butter, room temperature
4 large eggs
1 tablespoon vanilla extract, optional

TOPPING:
1 cup heavy cream
1 teaspoon vanilla extract
2 tablespoons granulated sugar

GARNISH:
Chocolate shards

Preheat oven to 350 degrees. Line a 5-cup oven-proof bowl with a double thickness of foil.

Melt the chocolate with the water and sugar over low heat or in the microwave; cool slightly.

Transfer the chocolate mixture to a mixing bowl or to a food processor bowl fitted with the knife blade. Beat in the butter, add the eggs one by one, followed by the vanilla extract, beating after each addition.

Pour the mixture into the foil-lined mold; bake 1 hour or until a thick crust has formed on top. It will still be soft under the crust.

Remove from oven. It will collapse. Cool completely. Cover tightly and refrigerate until solid, 2 to 3 hours or overnight, or freeze. This can be done several days in advance.

When ready to serve, whip the cream, sugar, and vanilla until stiff, and move to a piping bag with a star tip. Remove the snowball from the bowl and peel off the foil.

Place on a serving dish, flat side down.

Pipe rosettes of whipped cream over the entire surface until no chocolate shows. Chill until served. Garnish with chocolate shavings if desired. Leftovers freeze well, tightly wrapped—good enough for family anyway.

A Lowcountry Christmas

The key to this recipe is a nice acid-sweet balance. Use good cider!

To make an individual drink . . .

2 ounces apple pie moonshine
4 to 6 ounces apple cider
Juice of one half lemon

FOR A BATCH:
1 bottle Firefly apple pie moonshine
2 bottles apple cider
½ container of lemon juice (1 cup)

Warm it up in a beverage warmer. Putting on the stove top lends an aroma throughout one's house that will leave you weeping with delight!